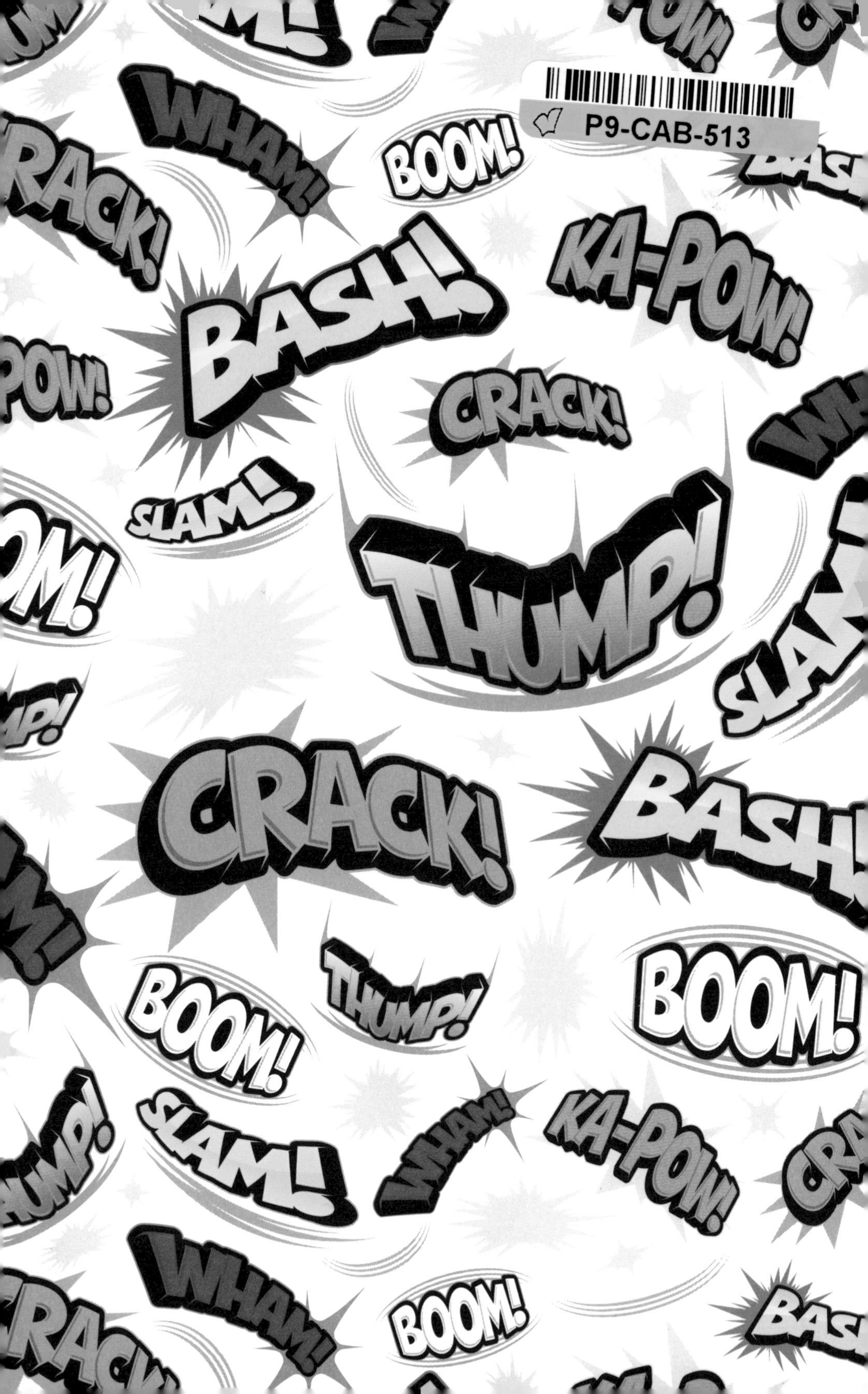
WHAM!
BOOM!
KA-POW!
BASH!
CRACK!
SLAM!
THUMP!
CRACK!
BASH!
BOOM!
THUMP!
BOOM!
SLAM!
WHAM!
KA-POW!
WHAM!
BOOM!

WWE SLAM CITY

PAPERCUTZ

OTHER GREAT GRAPHIC NOVELS AVAILABLE FROM PAPERCUTZ

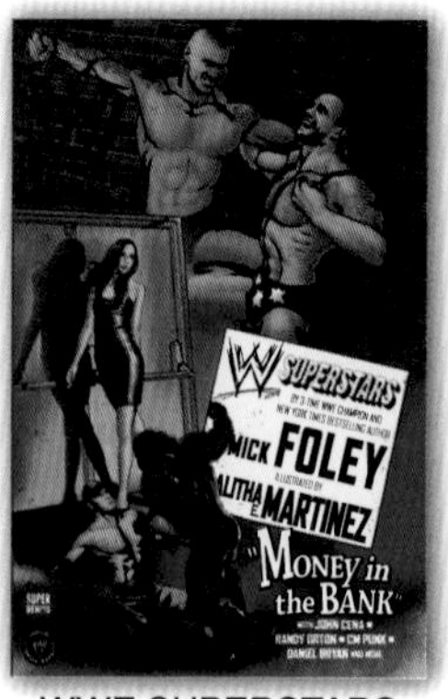
WWE SUPERSTARS
MICK FOLEY
ALITHA MARTINEZ
"Money in the BANK"

WWE SUPERSTARS #1

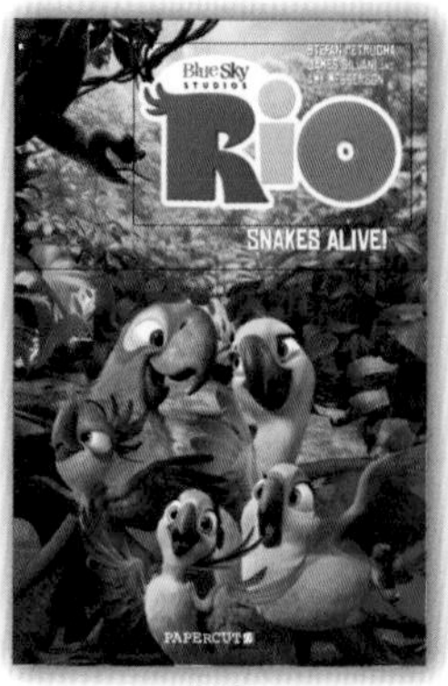
Blue Sky STUDIOS
RIO
SNAKES ALIVE!
PAPERCUTZ

RIO #1

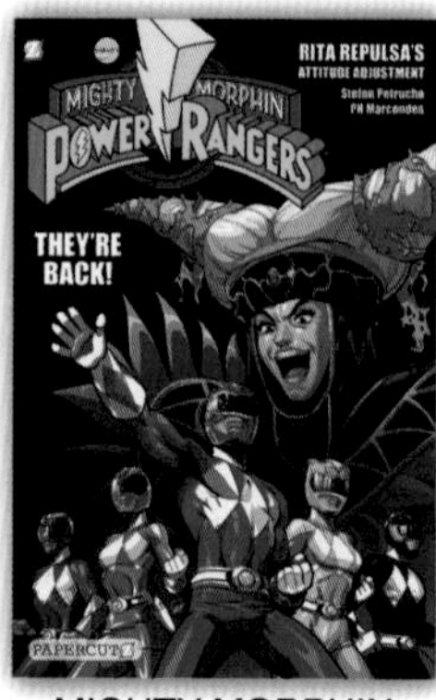
RITA REPULSA'S ATTITUDE ADJUSTMENT
MIGHTY MORPHIN POWER RANGERS
THEY'RE BACK!
PAPERCUTZ

MIGHTY MORPHIN POWER RANGERS #1

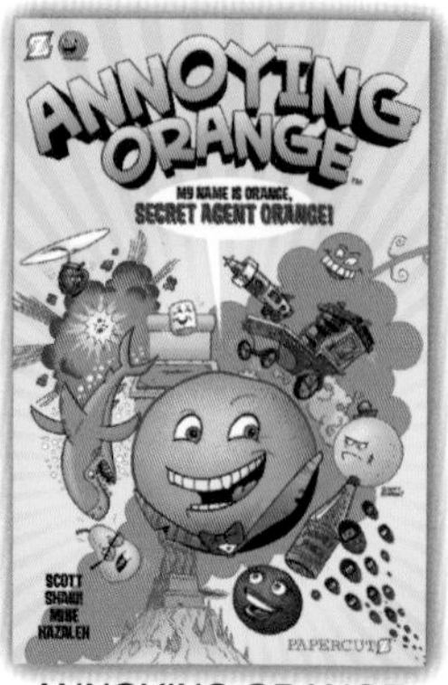
ANNOYING ORANGE
MY NAME IS ORANGE, SECRET AGENT ORANGE!
PAPERCUTZ

ANNOYING ORANGE #1

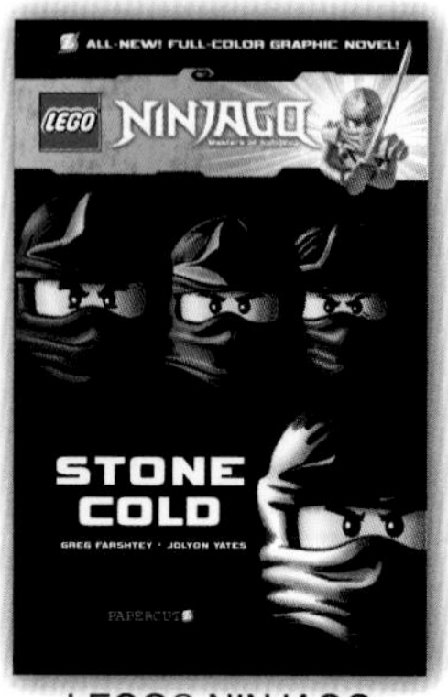
ALL-NEW! FULL-COLOR GRAPHIC NOVEL!
LEGO NINJAGO
STONE COLD
GREG FARSHTEY · JOLYON YATES
PAPERCUTZ

LEGO® NINJAGO #7

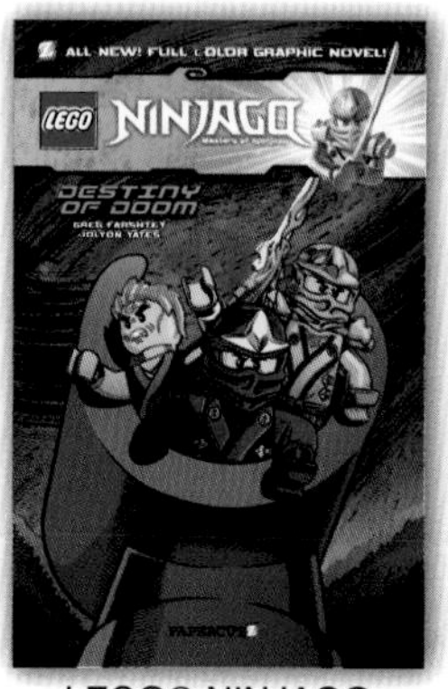
LEGO NINJAGO
DESTINY OF DOOM
GREG FARSHTEY
JOLYON YATES

LEGO® NINJAGO #8

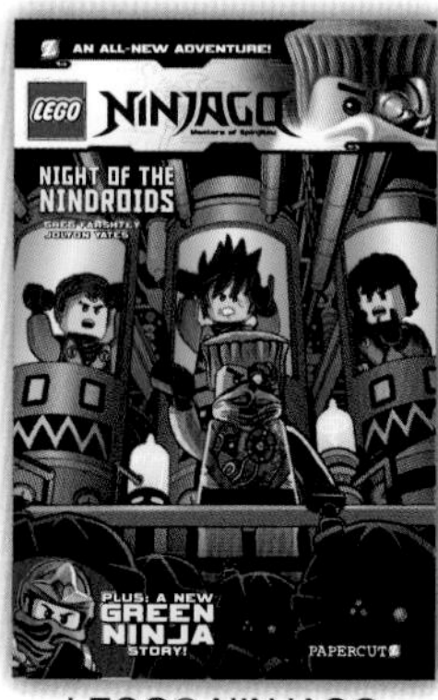
AN ALL-NEW ADVENTURE!
LEGO NINJAGO
NIGHT OF THE NINDROIDS
PLUS: A NEW GREEN NINJA STORY!
PAPERCUTZ

LEGO® NINJAGO #9

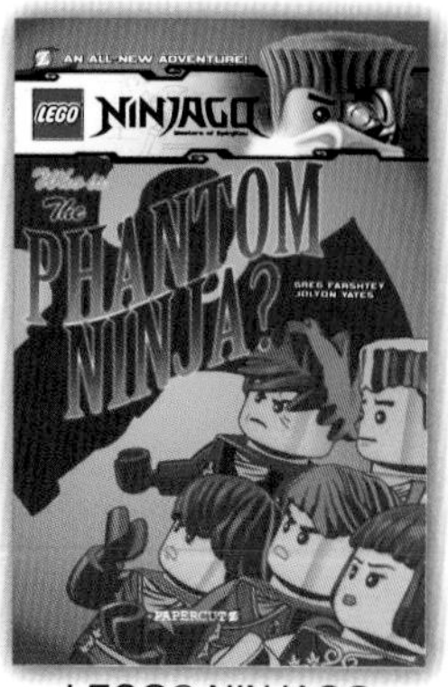
AN ALL-NEW ADVENTURE!
LEGO NINJAGO
the PHANTOM NINJA?
PAPERCUTZ

LEGO® NINJAGO #10

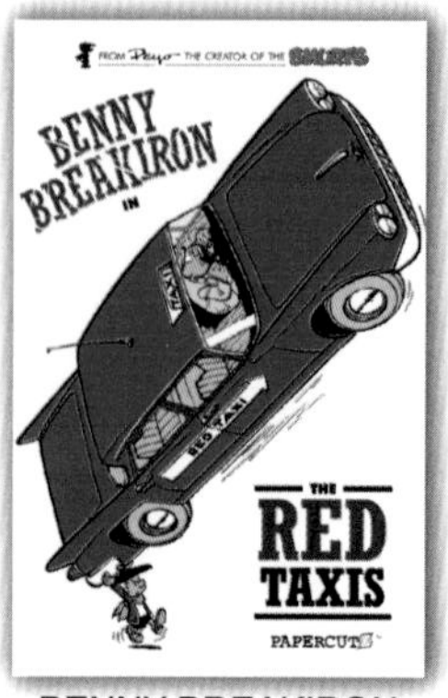
BENNY BREAKIRON IN
THE RED TAXIS
PAPERCUTZ

BENNY BREAKIRON #1

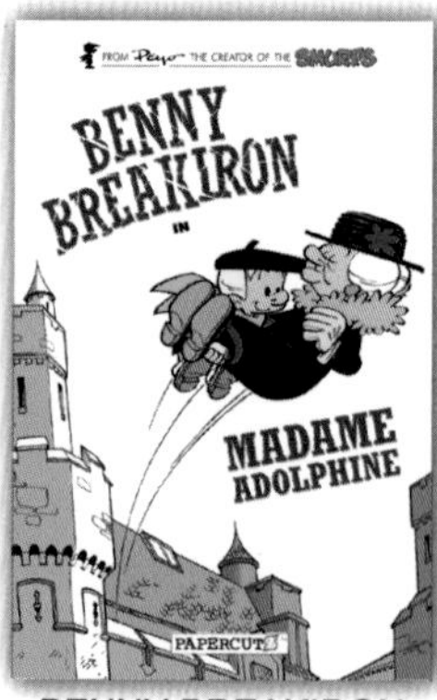
BENNY BREAKIRON IN
MADAME ADOLPHINE
PAPERCUTZ

BENNY BREAKIRON #2

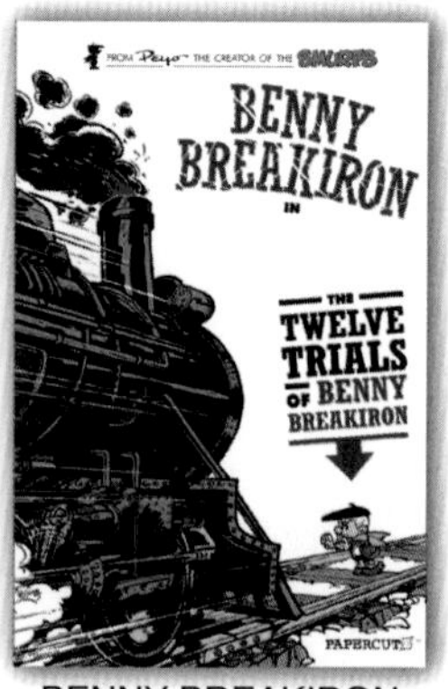
BENNY BREAKIRON IN
THE TWELVE TRIALS OF BENNY BREAKIRON
PAPERCUTZ

BENNY BREAKIRON #3

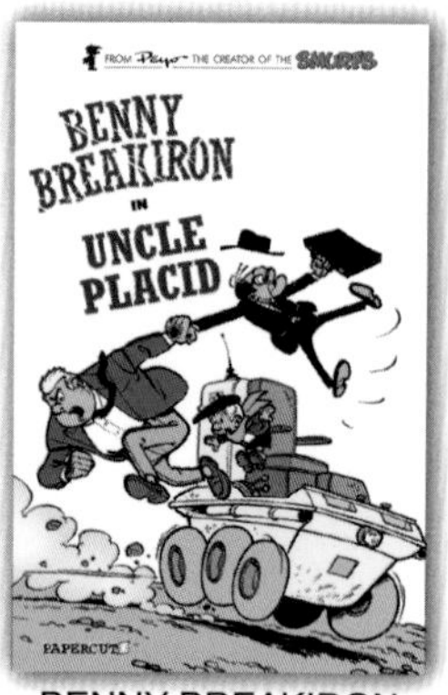
BENNY BREAKIRON IN
UNCLE PLACID
PAPERCUTZ

BENNY BREAKIRON #4

WWE SUPERSTARS is $9.99 in paperback only; RIO is $7.99 in paperback and $11.99 in hardcover; MIGHTY MORPHIN POWER RANGERS is $7.99 in paperback and $11.99 in hardcover; ANNOYING ORANGE is $6.99 in paperback and $10.99 in hardcover; LEGO NINJAGO is $6.99 each in paperback and $10.99 each in hardcover; and BENNY BREAKIRON is $11.99 each in hardcover only, at booksellers everywhere. You can also order online at papercutz.com. Or call 1-800-886-1223, Monday through Friday, 9 – 5 EST. MC, Visa, and AmEx accepted. To order by mail, please add $4.00 for postage and handling for first book ordered, $1.00 for each additional book and make check payable to NBM Publishing. Send to: Papercutz, 160 Broadway, Suite 700, East Wing, New York, NY 10038.

Papercutz graphic novels are also available digitally wherever e-books are sold.

WWE SLAM CITY

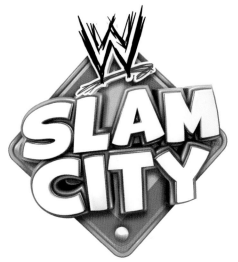

#1 "FINISHED!"

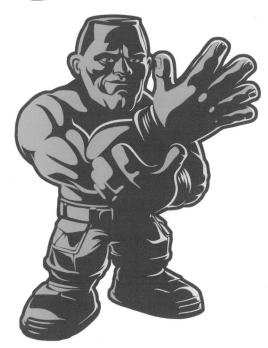

Mathias Triton – Writer

Alitha E. Martinez – Artist

JayJay Jackson – Colorist

PAPERCUTZ™

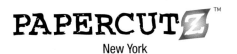

New York

WWE SLAM CITY
#1 "Finished!"

Mathias Triton – Writer
Alitha E. Martinez – Artist
Jolyon Yates – Cover Artist
JayJay Jackson – Colorist
Tom Orzechowski – Letterer
Dawn K. Guzzo – Production
Beth Scorzato – Production Coordinator
Michael Petranek – Associate Editor
Eric Lyga, Steven Pantaleo – Special Thanks

Jim Salicrup
Editor-in-Chief

ISBN: 978-1-59707-721-7 paperback edition
ISBN: 978-1-59707-722-4 hardcover edition

Papercutz books may be purchased for business or promotional use. For information on bulk purchases please contact Macmillan Corporate and Premium Sales Department at (800) 221-7945 x5442.

Printed in the USA
August 2014 by Lifetouch Printing
5126 Forest Hills Ct.
Loves Park, IL 61111

Distributed by Macmillan
First Printing

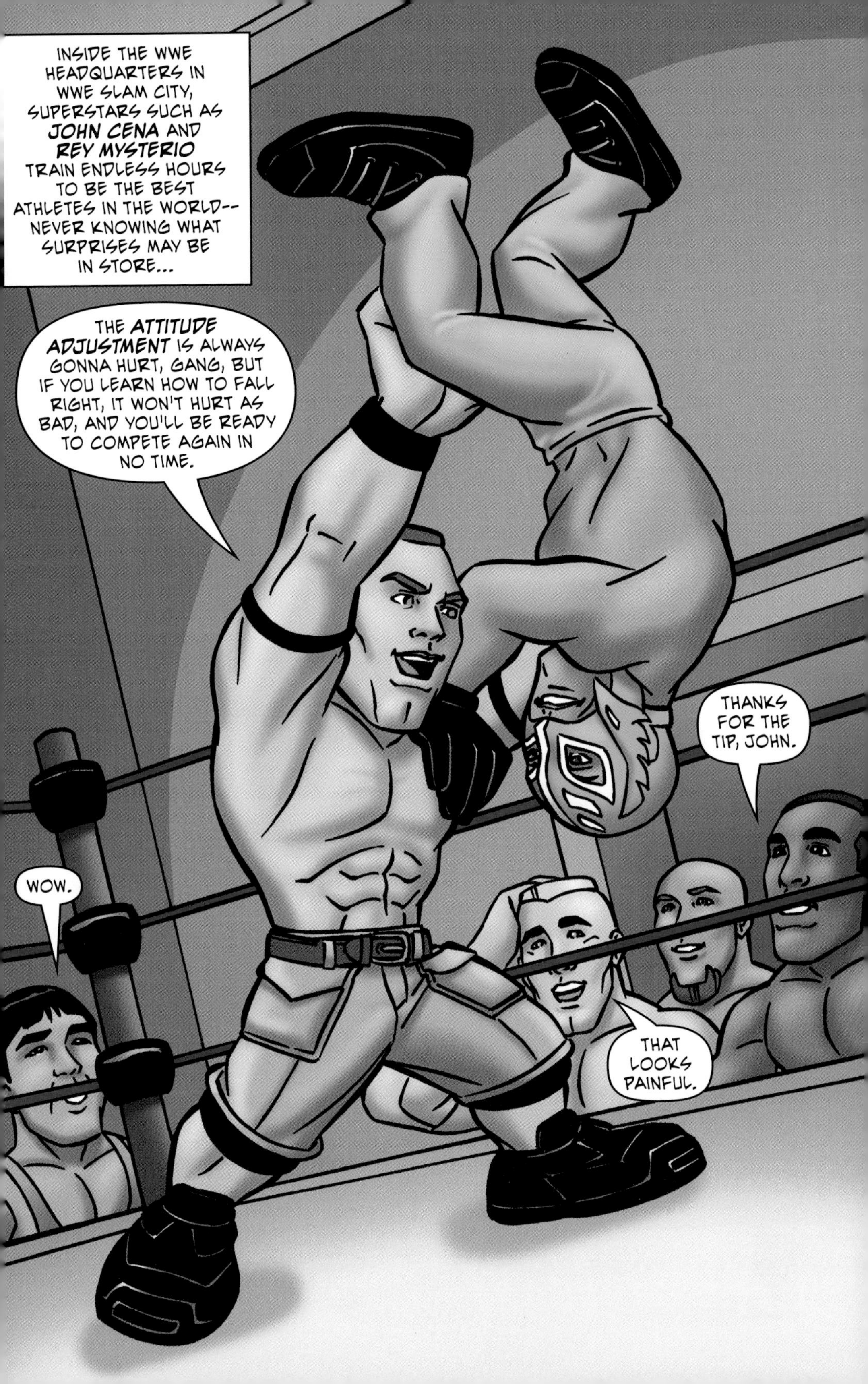
INSIDE THE WWE HEADQUARTERS IN WWE SLAM CITY, SUPERSTARS SUCH AS **JOHN CENA** AND **REY MYSTERIO** TRAIN ENDLESS HOURS TO BE THE BEST ATHLETES IN THE WORLD--NEVER KNOWING WHAT SURPRISES MAY BE IN STORE...
THE **ATTITUDE ADJUSTMENT** IS ALWAYS GONNA HURT, GANG, BUT IF YOU LEARN HOW TO FALL RIGHT, IT WON'T HURT AS BAD, AND YOU'LL BE READY TO COMPETE AGAIN IN NO TIME.
THANKS FOR THE TIP, JOHN.
WOW.
THAT LOOKS PAINFUL.

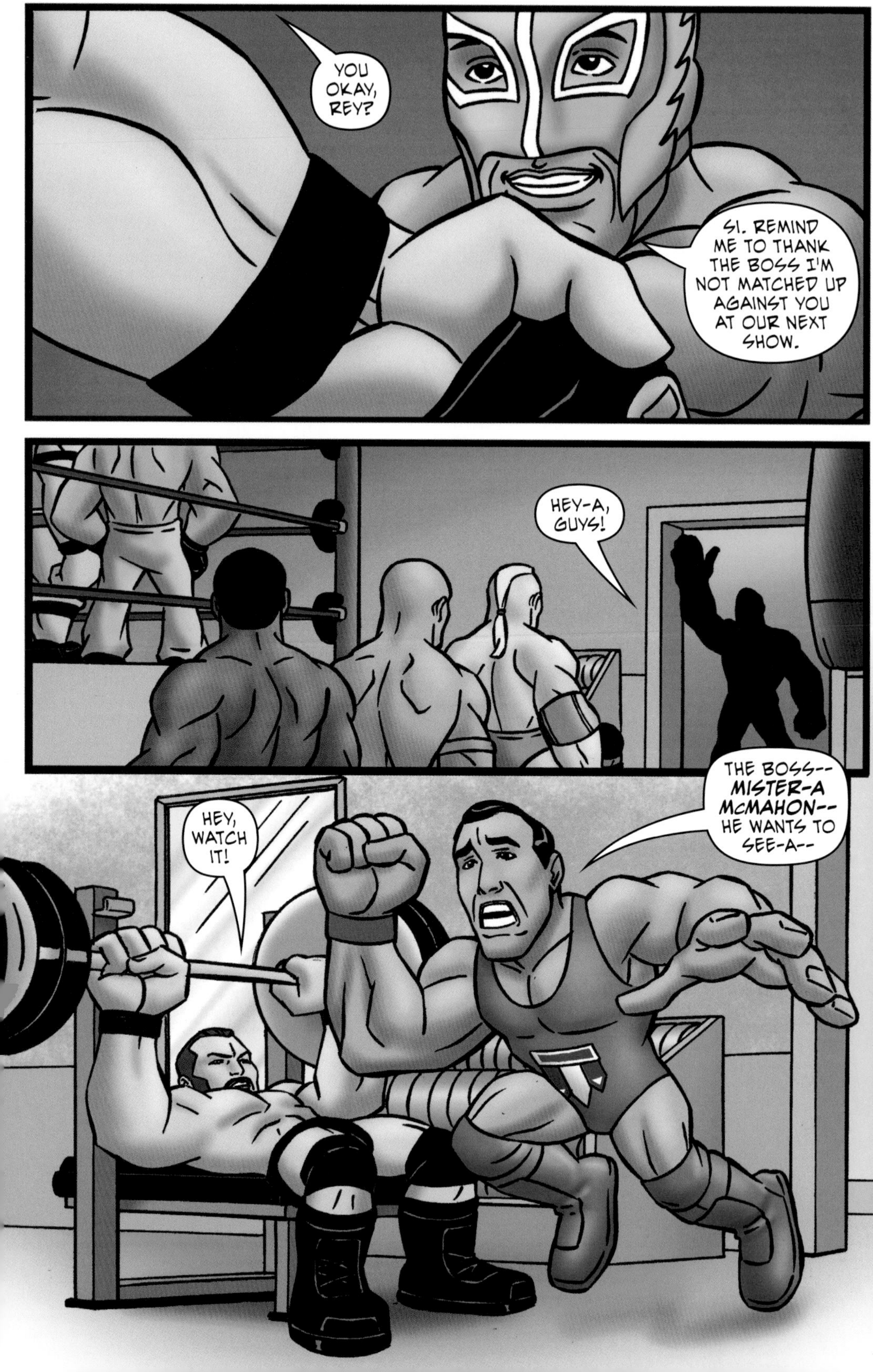
YOU OKAY, REY?
SI. REMIND ME TO THANK THE BOSS I'M NOT MATCHED UP AGAINST YOU AT OUR NEXT SHOW.
HEY-A, GUYS!
THE BOSS-- MISTER-A McMAHON-- HE WANTS TO SEE-A--
HEY, WATCH IT!

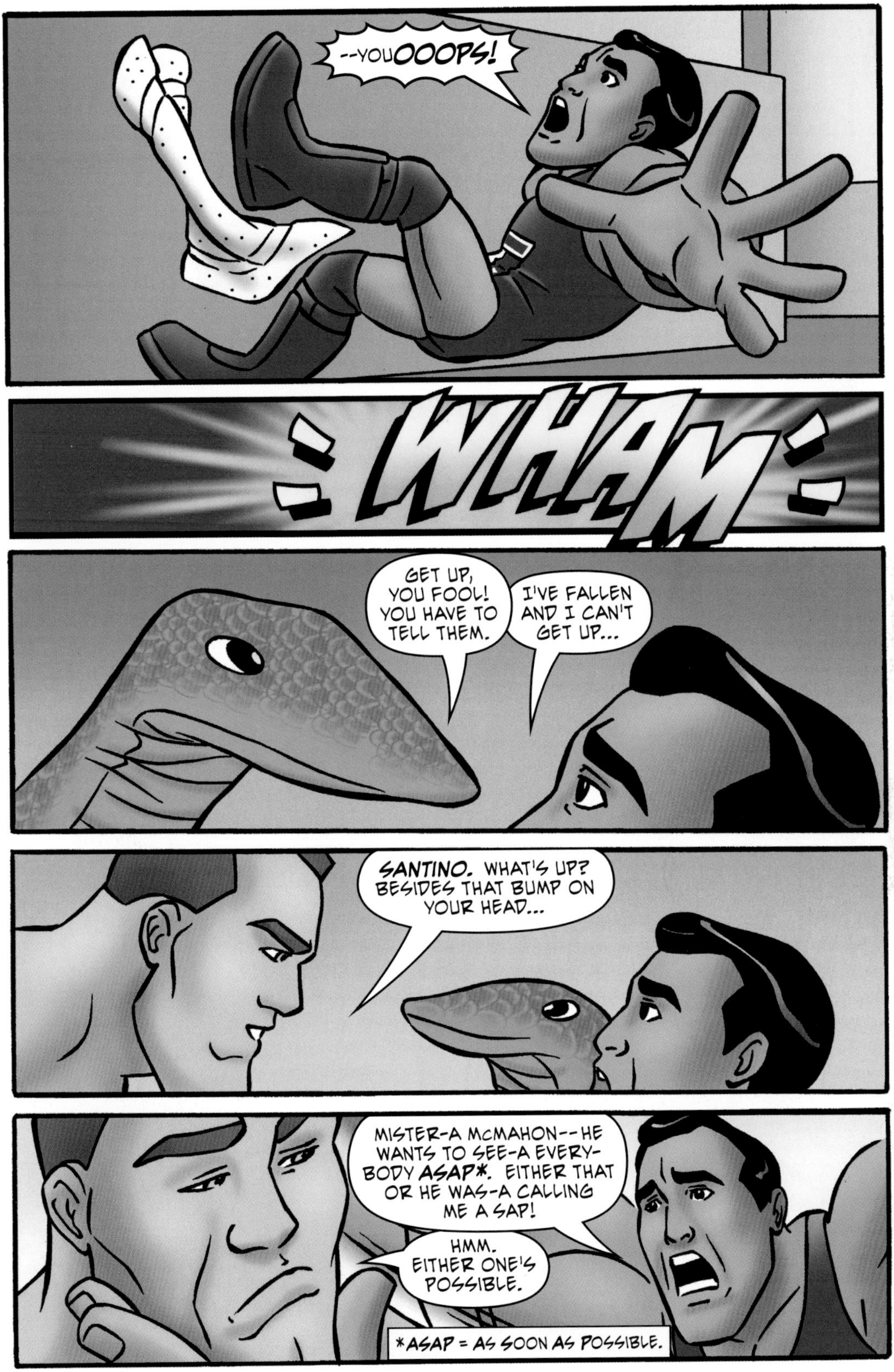
--YOU OOOPS!
WHAM
GET UP, YOU FOOL! YOU HAVE TO TELL THEM.
I'VE FALLEN AND I CAN'T GET UP...
SANTINO. WHAT'S UP? BESIDES THAT BUMP ON YOUR HEAD...
MISTER-A McMAHON--HE WANTS TO SEE-A EVERY-BODY ASAP*. EITHER THAT OR HE WAS-A CALLING ME A SAP!
HMM. EITHER ONE'S POSSIBLE.
*ASAP = AS SOON AS POSSIBLE.

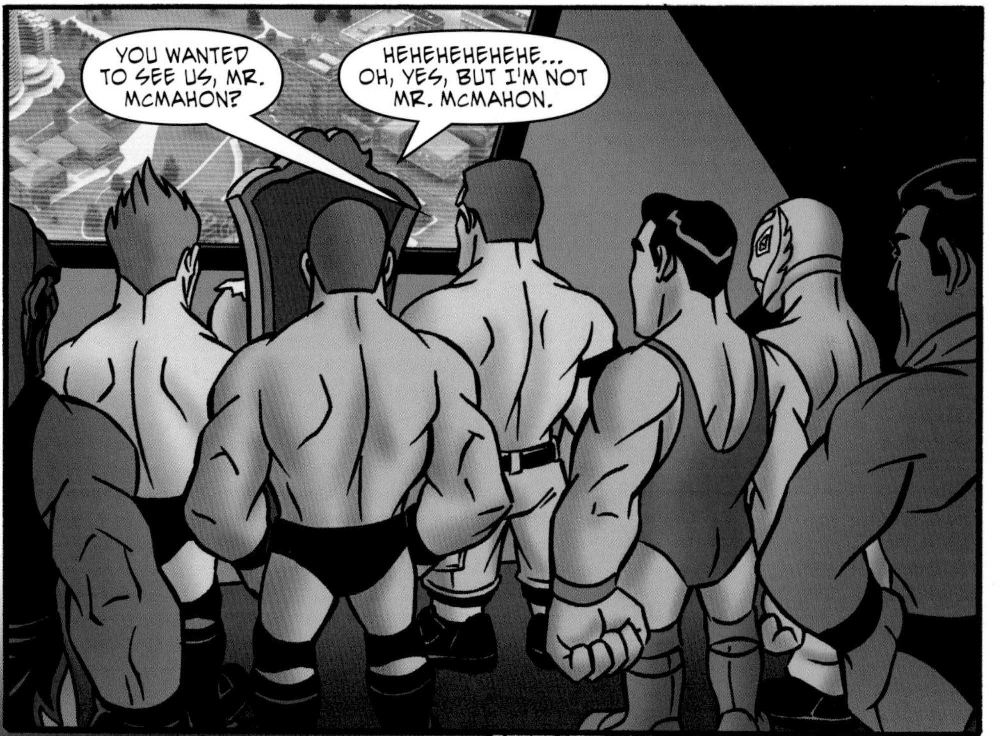
YOU WANTED TO SEE US, MR. MCMAHON?
HEHEHEHEHEHE... OH, YES, BUT I'M NOT MR. MCMAHON.

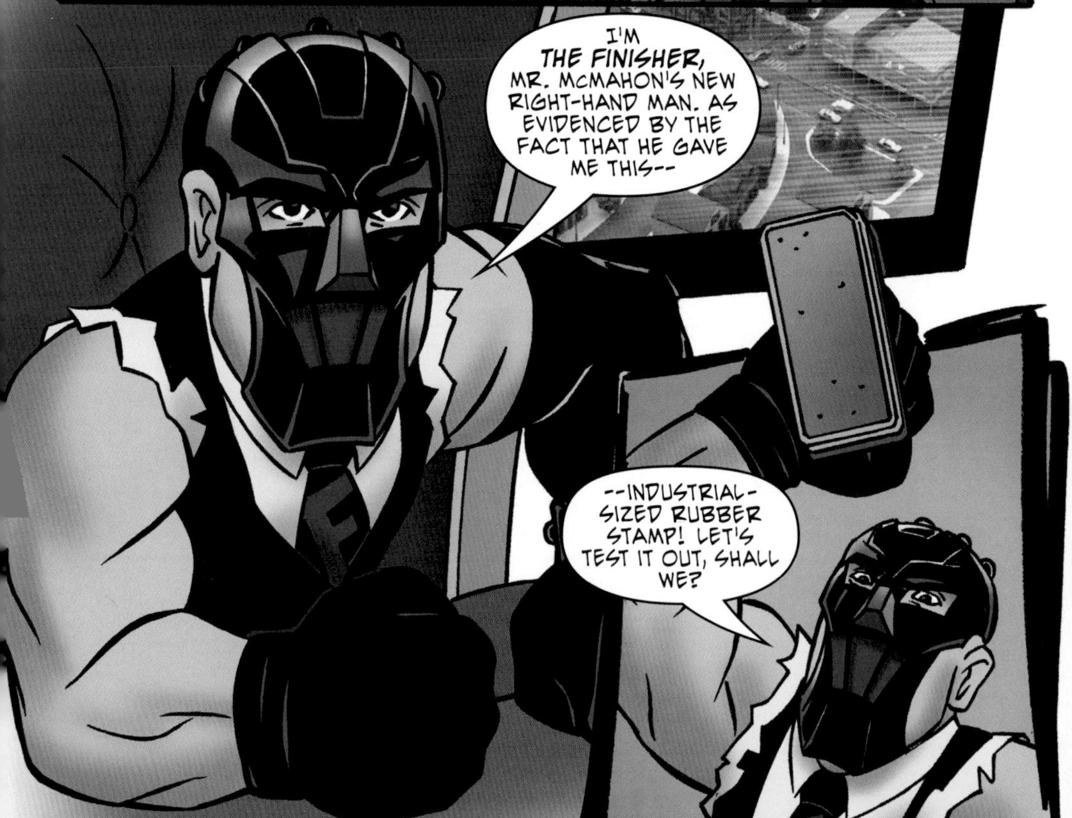
I'M THE FINISHER, MR. MCMAHON'S NEW RIGHT-HAND MAN. AS EVIDENCED BY THE FACT THAT HE GAVE ME THIS--
--INDUSTRIAL-SIZED RUBBER STAMP! LET'S TEST IT OUT, SHALL WE?

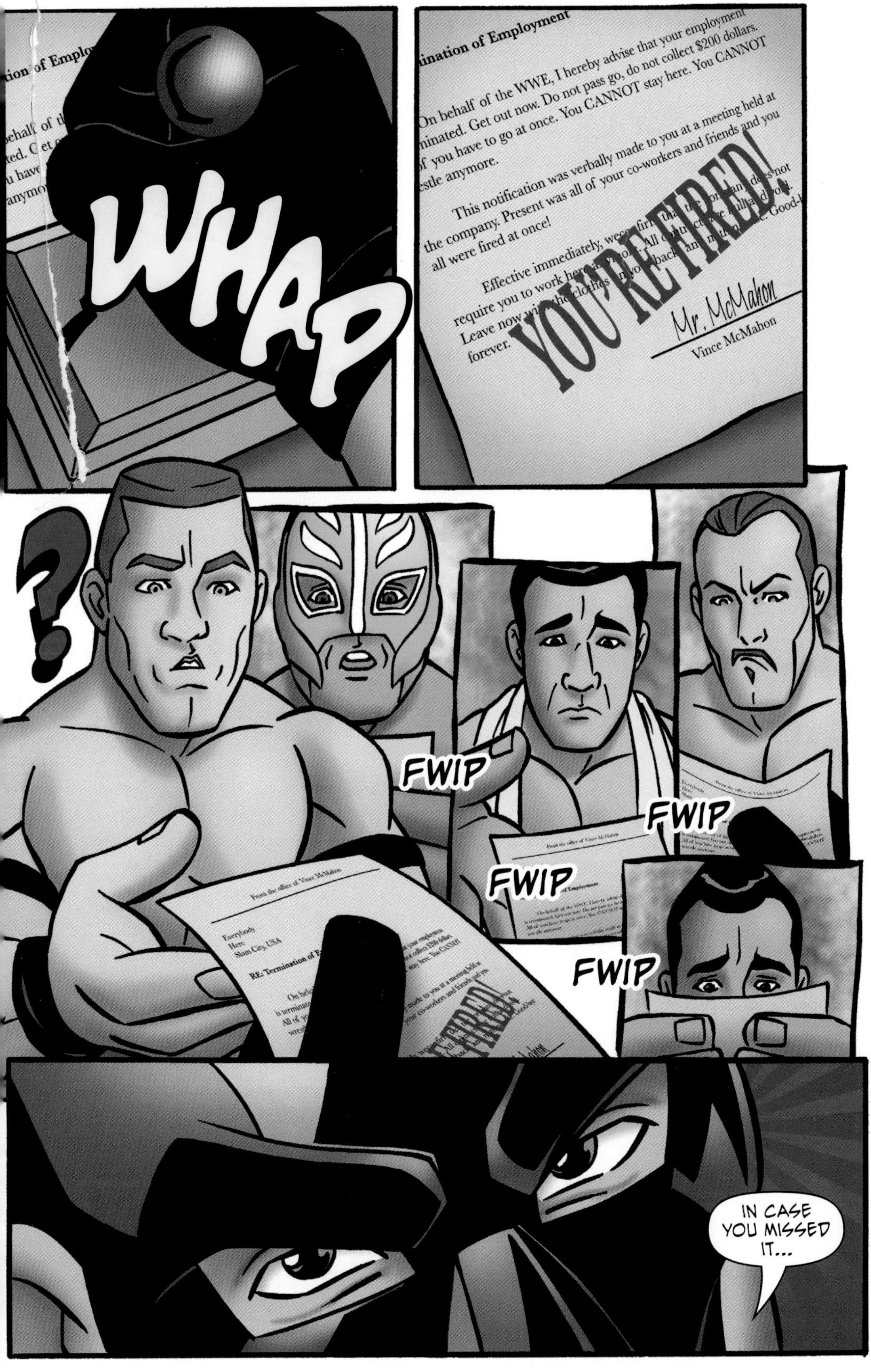
WHAP
ination of Employment
On behalf of the WWE, I hereby advise that your employment
minated. Get out now. Do not pass go, do not collect $200 dollars.
of you have to go at once. You CANNOT stay here. You CANNOT
estle anymore.
This notification was verbally made to you at a meeting held at
the company. Present was all of your co-workers and friends and you
all were fired at once!
YOU'RE FIRED!
Mr. McMahon
Vince McMahon
FWIP
FWIP
FWIP
FWIP
IN CASE YOU MISSED IT...

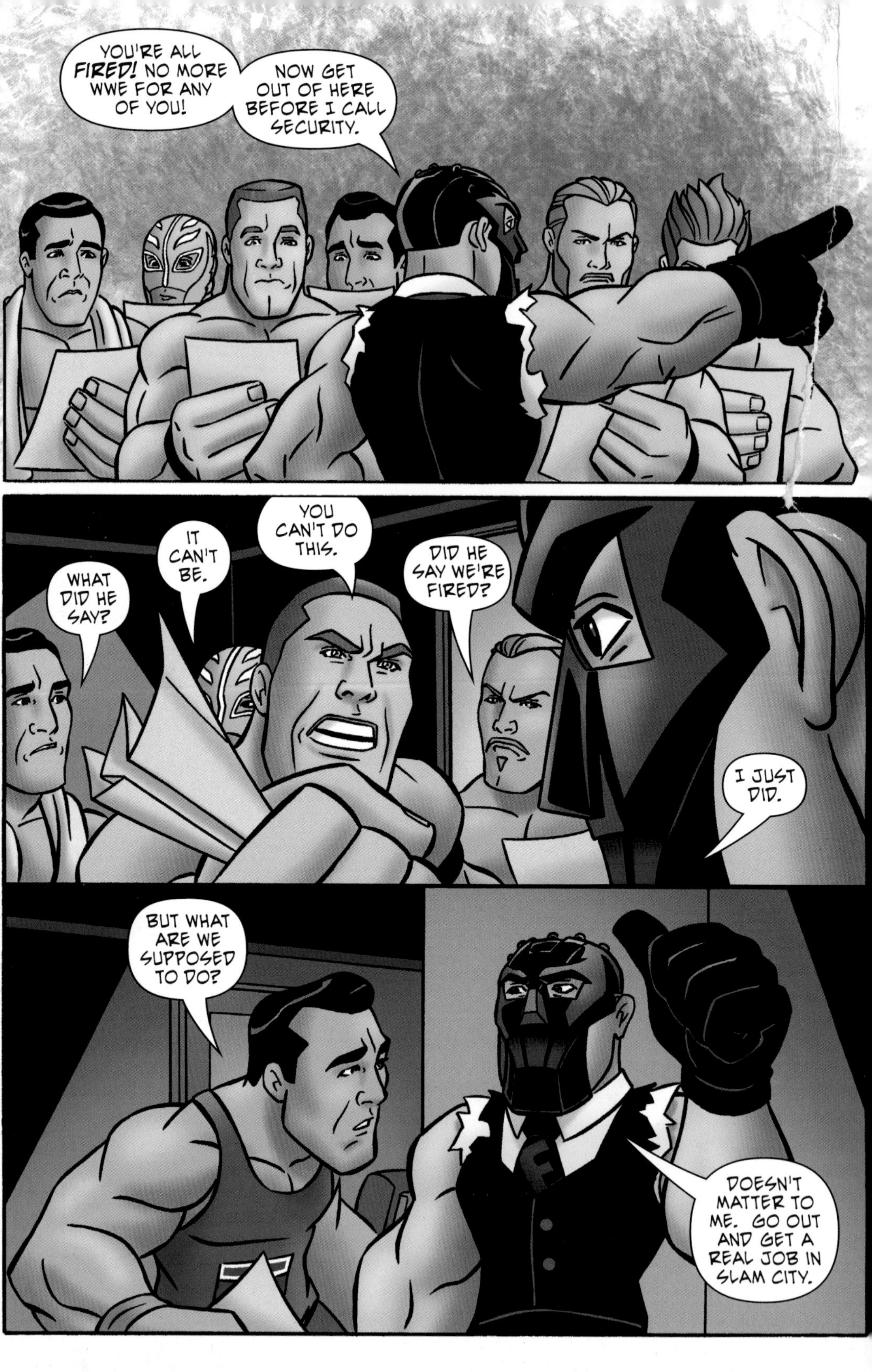
YOU'RE ALL FIRED! NO MORE WWE FOR ANY OF YOU!
NOW GET OUT OF HERE BEFORE I CALL SECURITY.
WHAT DID HE SAY?
IT CAN'T BE.
YOU CAN'T DO THIS.
DID HE SAY WE'RE FIRED?
I JUST DID.
BUT WHAT ARE WE SUPPOSED TO DO?
DOESN'T MATTER TO ME. GO OUT AND GET A REAL JOB IN SLAM CITY.

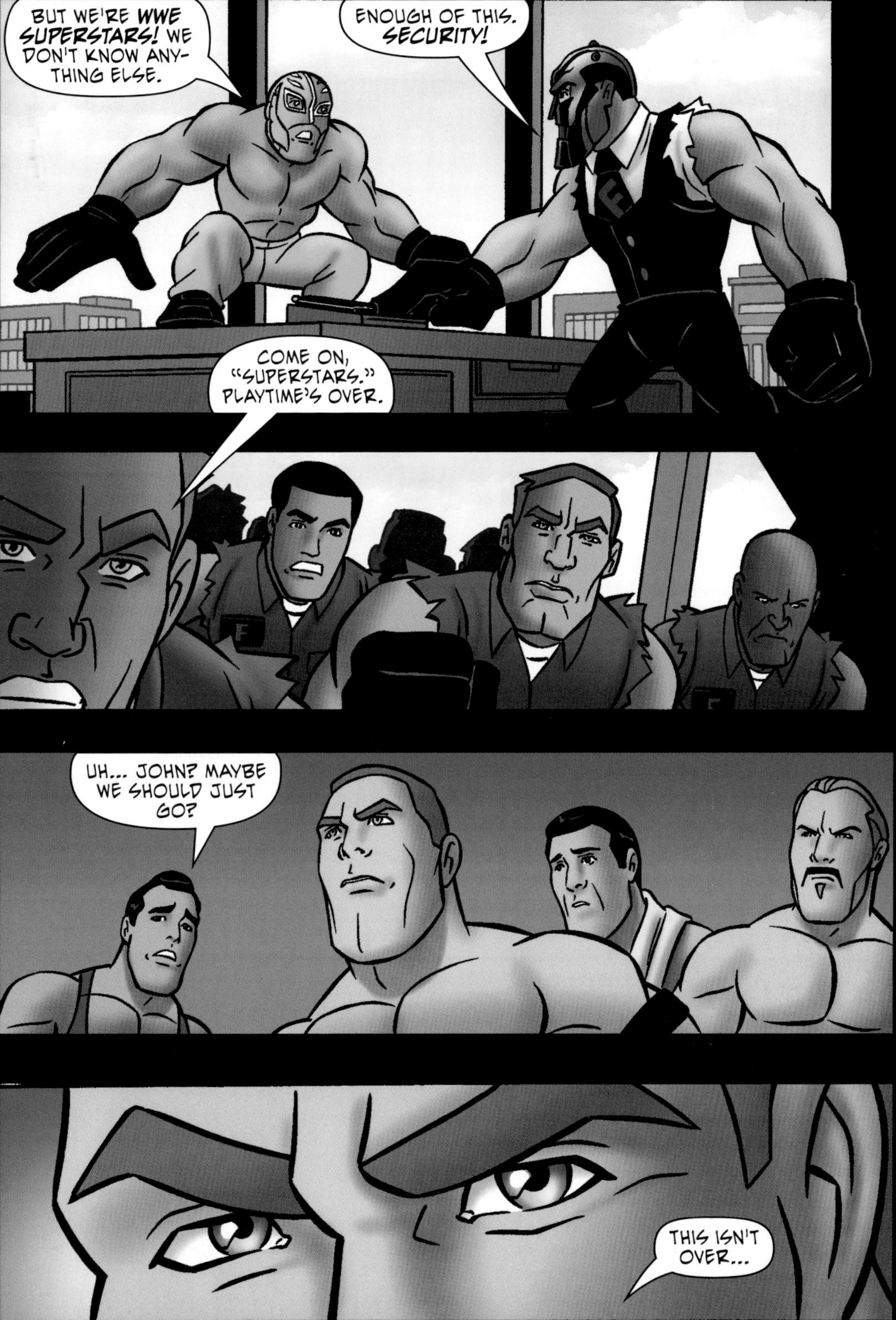

BUT WE'RE **WWE SUPERSTARS!** WE DON'T KNOW ANYTHING ELSE.
ENOUGH OF THIS. **SECURITY!**
COME ON, "SUPERSTARS." PLAYTIME'S OVER.
UH... JOHN? MAYBE WE SHOULD JUST GO?
THIS ISN'T OVER...

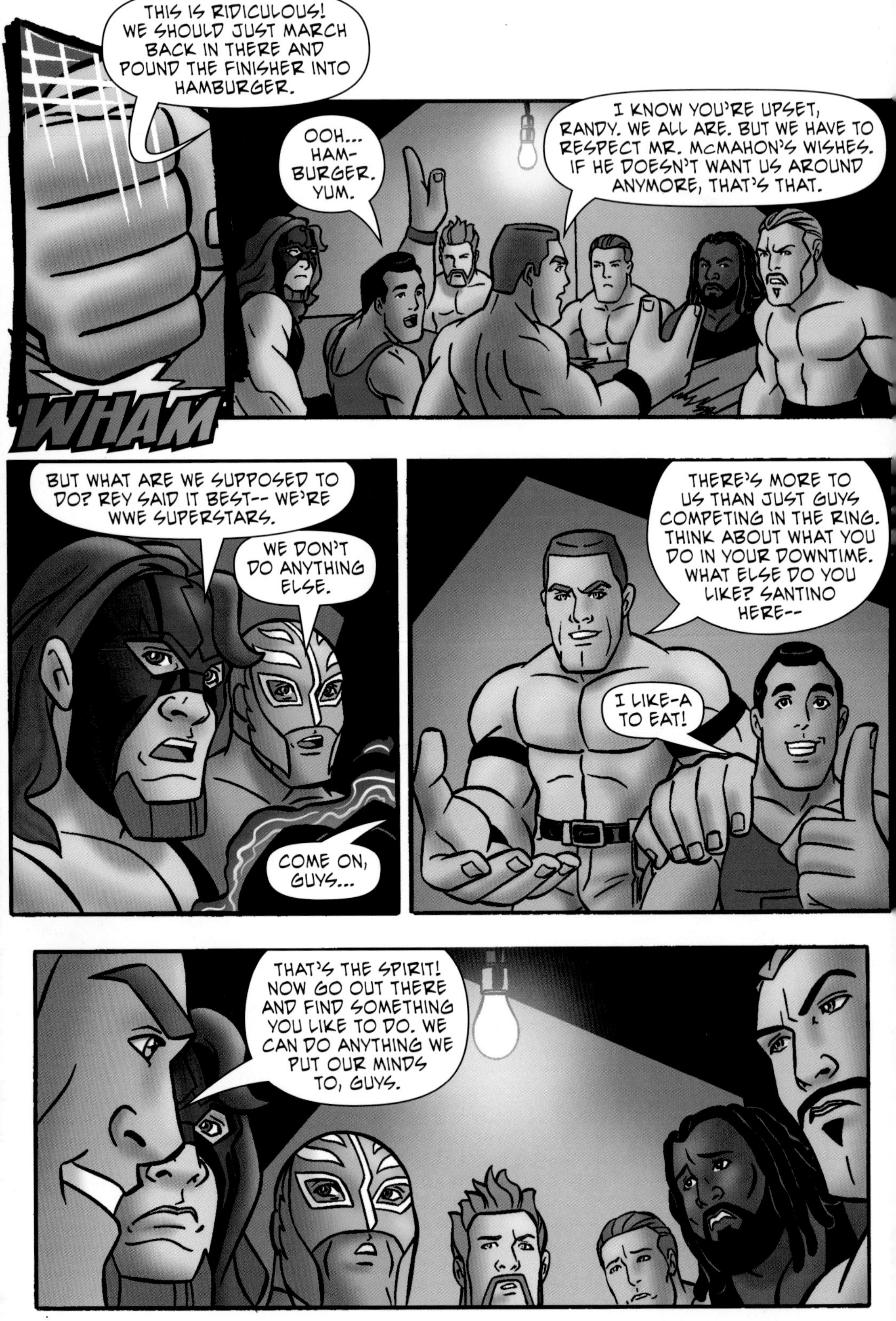
THIS IS RIDICULOUS! WE SHOULD JUST MARCH BACK IN THERE AND POUND THE FINISHER INTO HAMBURGER.
WHAM
OOH... HAM-BURGER. YUM.
I KNOW YOU'RE UPSET, RANDY. WE ALL ARE. BUT WE HAVE TO RESPECT MR. McMAHON'S WISHES. IF HE DOESN'T WANT US AROUND ANYMORE, THAT'S THAT.
BUT WHAT ARE WE SUPPOSED TO DO? REY SAID IT BEST-- WE'RE WWE SUPERSTARS.
WE DON'T DO ANYTHING ELSE.
COME ON, GUYS...
THERE'S MORE TO US THAN JUST GUYS COMPETING IN THE RING. THINK ABOUT WHAT YOU DO IN YOUR DOWNTIME. WHAT ELSE DO YOU LIKE? SANTINO HERE--
I LIKE-A TO EAT!
THAT'S THE SPIRIT! NOW GO OUT THERE AND FIND SOMETHING YOU LIKE TO DO. WE CAN DO ANYTHING WE PUT OUR MINDS TO, GUYS.

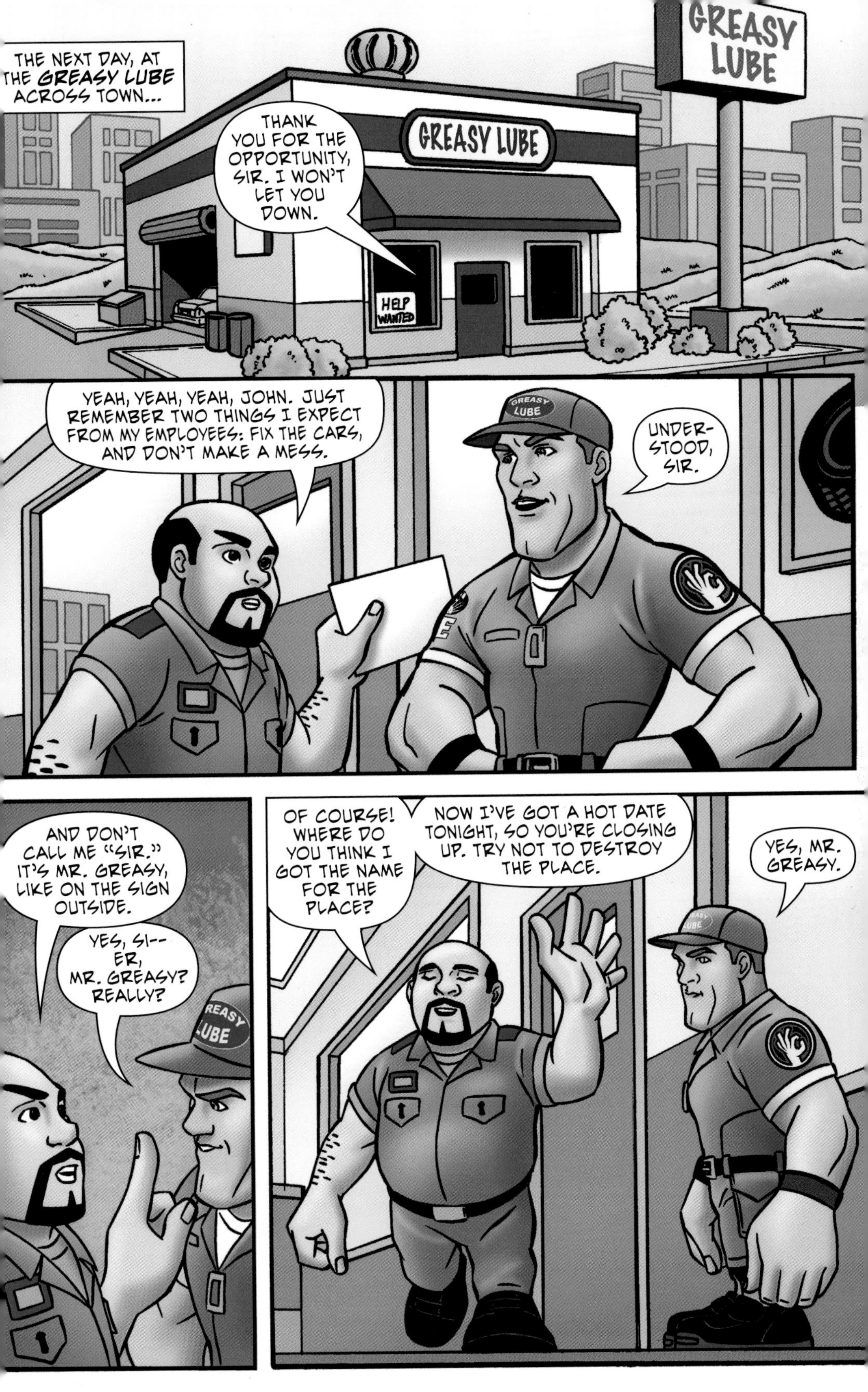
THE NEXT DAY, AT THE *GREASY LUBE* ACROSS TOWN...
GREASY LUBE
GREASY LUBE
THANK YOU FOR THE OPPORTUNITY, SIR. I WON'T LET YOU DOWN.
HELP WANTED
YEAH, YEAH, YEAH, JOHN. JUST REMEMBER TWO THINGS I EXPECT FROM MY EMPLOYEES: FIX THE CARS, AND DON'T MAKE A MESS.
GREASY LUBE
UNDER-STOOD, SIR.
AND DON'T CALL ME "SIR." IT'S MR. GREASY, LIKE ON THE SIGN OUTSIDE.
YES, SI-- ER, MR. GREASY? REALLY?
GREASY LUBE
OF COURSE! WHERE DO YOU THINK I GOT THE NAME FOR THE PLACE?
NOW I'VE GOT A HOT DATE TONIGHT, SO YOU'RE CLOSING UP. TRY NOT TO DESTROY THE PLACE.
YES, MR. GREASY.

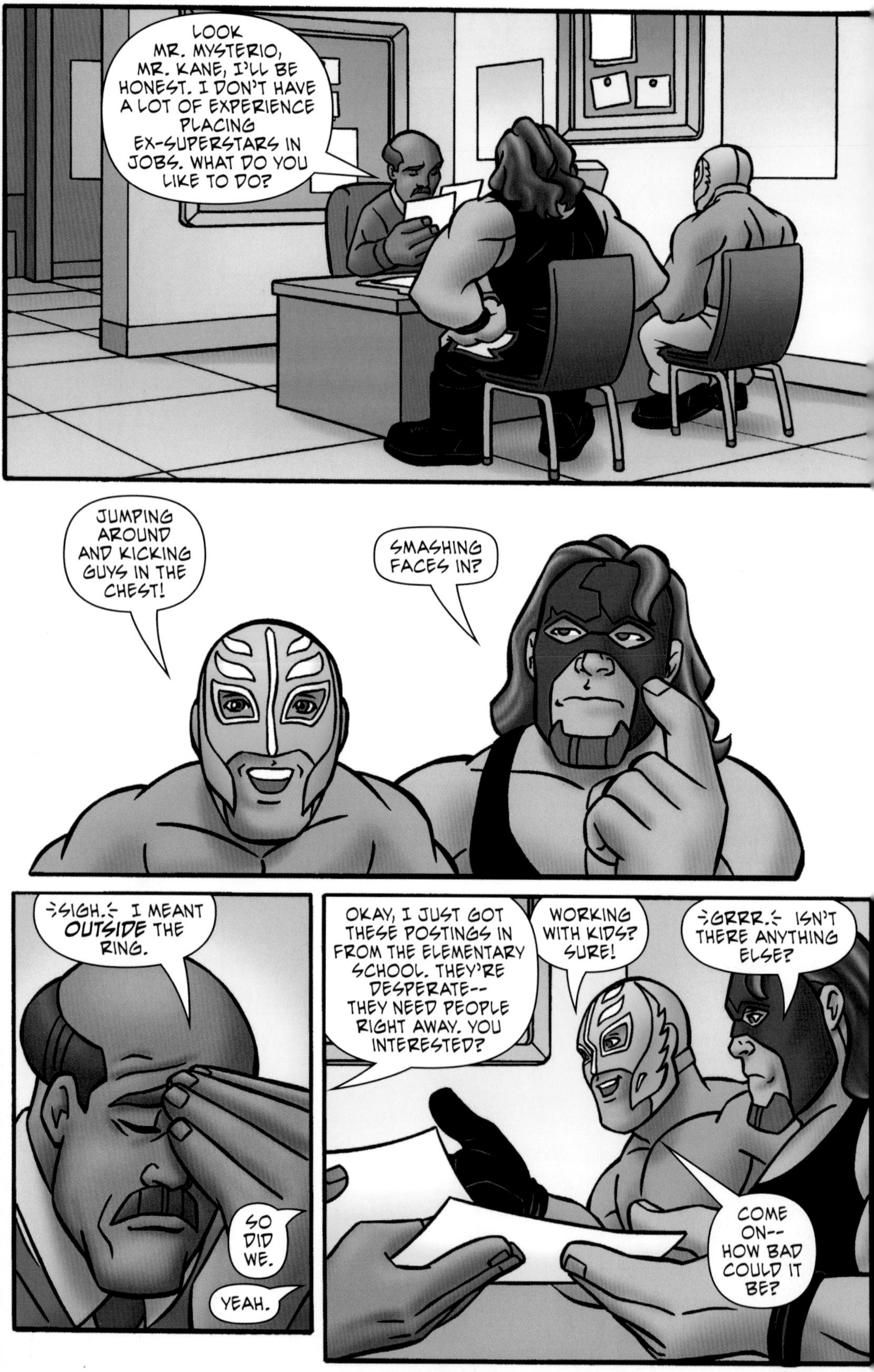
LOOK MR. MYSTERIO, MR. KANE, I'LL BE HONEST. I DON'T HAVE A LOT OF EXPERIENCE PLACING EX-SUPERSTARS IN JOBS. WHAT DO YOU LIKE TO DO?
JUMPING AROUND AND KICKING GUYS IN THE CHEST!
SMASHING FACES IN?
-SIGH.- I MEANT OUTSIDE THE RING.
SO DID WE.
YEAH.
OKAY, I JUST GOT THESE POSTINGS IN FROM THE ELEMENTARY SCHOOL. THEY'RE DESPERATE-- THEY NEED PEOPLE RIGHT AWAY. YOU INTERESTED?
WORKING WITH KIDS? SURE!
-GRRR.- ISN'T THERE ANYTHING ELSE?
COME ON-- HOW BAD COULD IT BE?

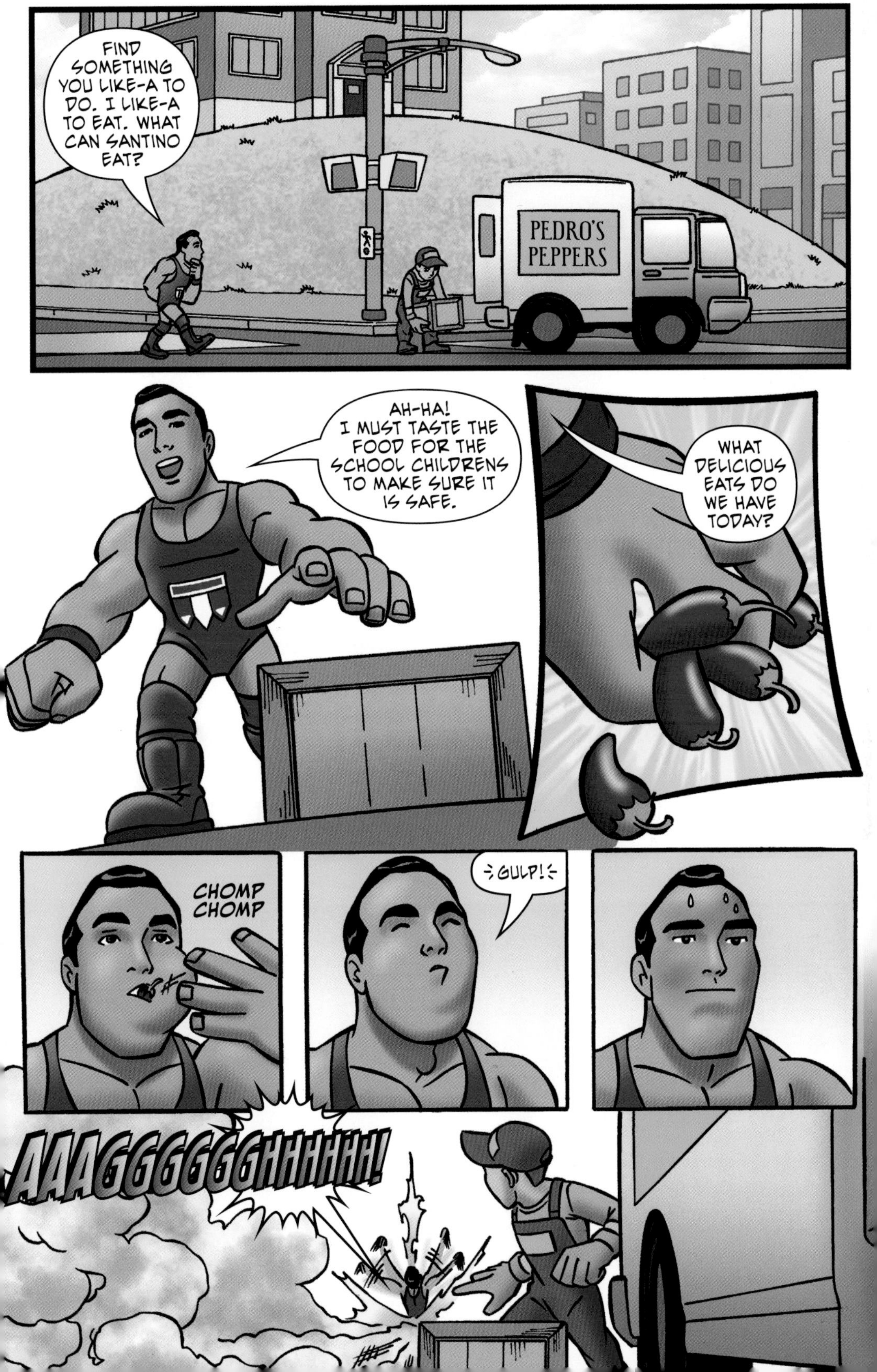
FIND SOMETHING YOU LIKE-A TO DO. I LIKE-A TO EAT. WHAT CAN SANTINO EAT?
PEDRO'S PEPPERS
AH-HA! I MUST TASTE THE FOOD FOR THE SCHOOL CHILDRENS TO MAKE SURE IT IS SAFE.
WHAT DELICIOUS EATS DO WE HAVE TODAY?
CHOMP CHOMP
GULP!
AAAGGGGGGHHHHHH!

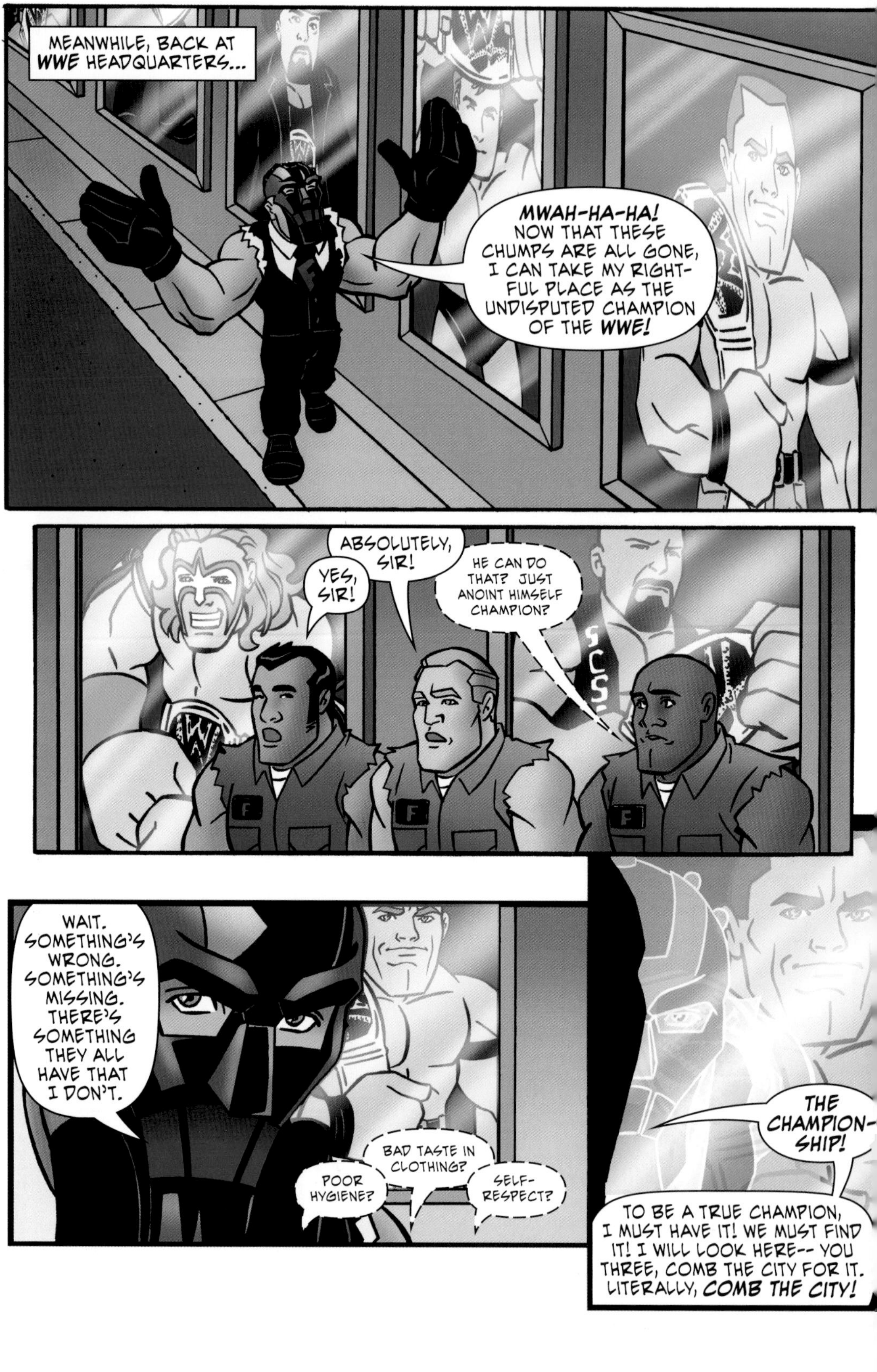
MEANWHILE, BACK AT WWE HEADQUARTERS...
MWAH-HA-HA! NOW THAT THESE CHUMPS ARE ALL GONE, I CAN TAKE MY RIGHTFUL PLACE AS THE UNDISPUTED CHAMPION OF THE WWE!
YES, SIR!
ABSOLUTELY, SIR!
HE CAN DO THAT? JUST ANOINT HIMSELF CHAMPION?
SCS
WAIT. SOMETHING'S WRONG. SOMETHING'S MISSING. THERE'S SOMETHING THEY ALL HAVE THAT I DON'T.
BAD TASTE IN CLOTHING?
POOR HYGIENE?
SELF-RESPECT?
THE CHAMPIONSHIP!
TO BE A TRUE CHAMPION, I MUST HAVE IT! WE MUST FIND IT! I WILL LOOK HERE-- YOU THREE, COMB THE CITY FOR IT. LITERALLY, COMB THE CITY!

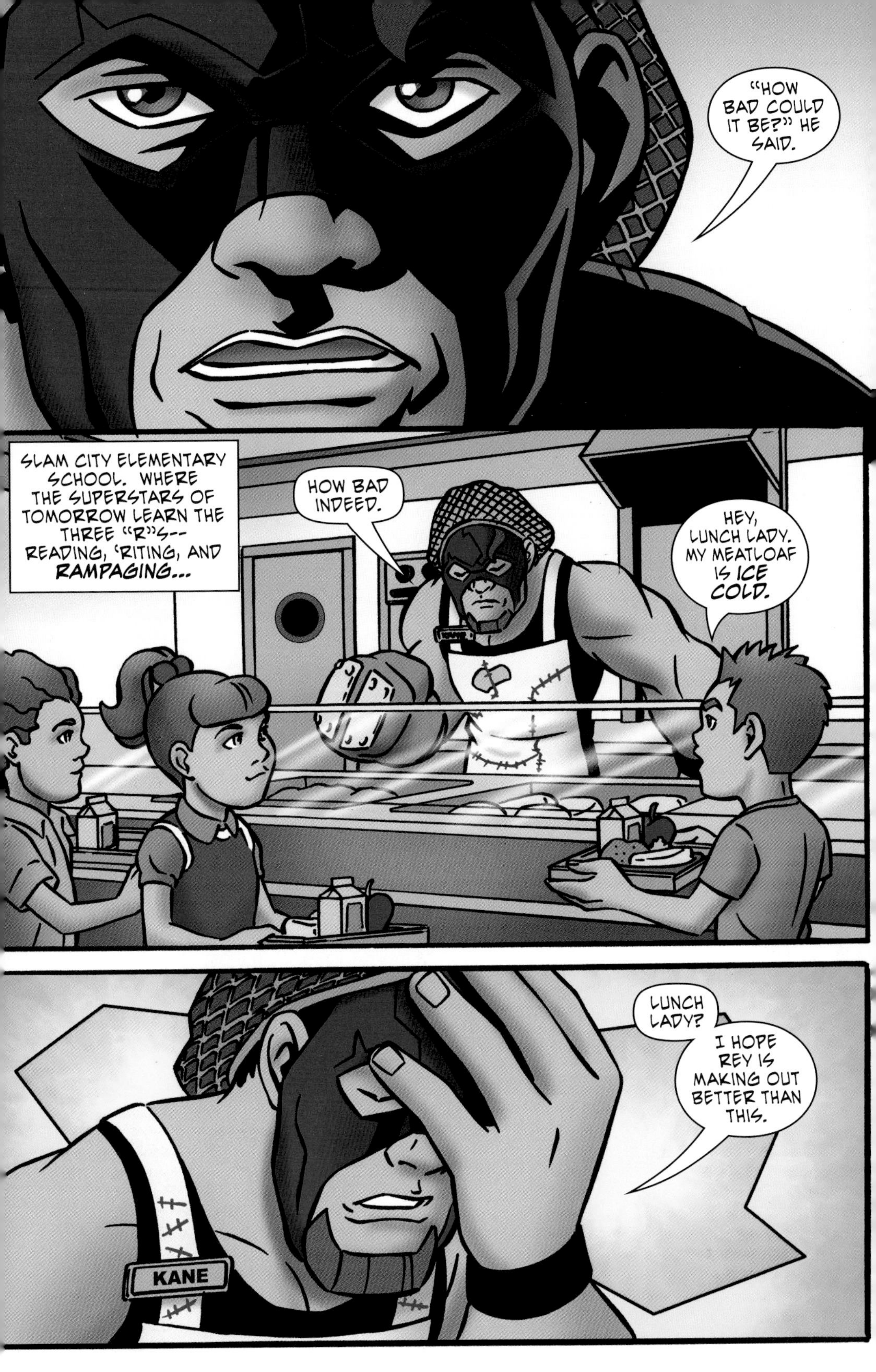
"HOW BAD COULD IT BE?" HE SAID.
SLAM CITY ELEMENTARY SCHOOL. WHERE THE SUPERSTARS OF TOMORROW LEARN THE THREE "R"S-- READING, 'RITING, AND **RAMPAGING...**
HOW BAD INDEED.
HEY, LUNCH LADY. MY MEATLOAF IS *ICE COLD.*
LUNCH LADY?
I HOPE REY IS MAKING OUT BETTER THAN THIS.
KANE

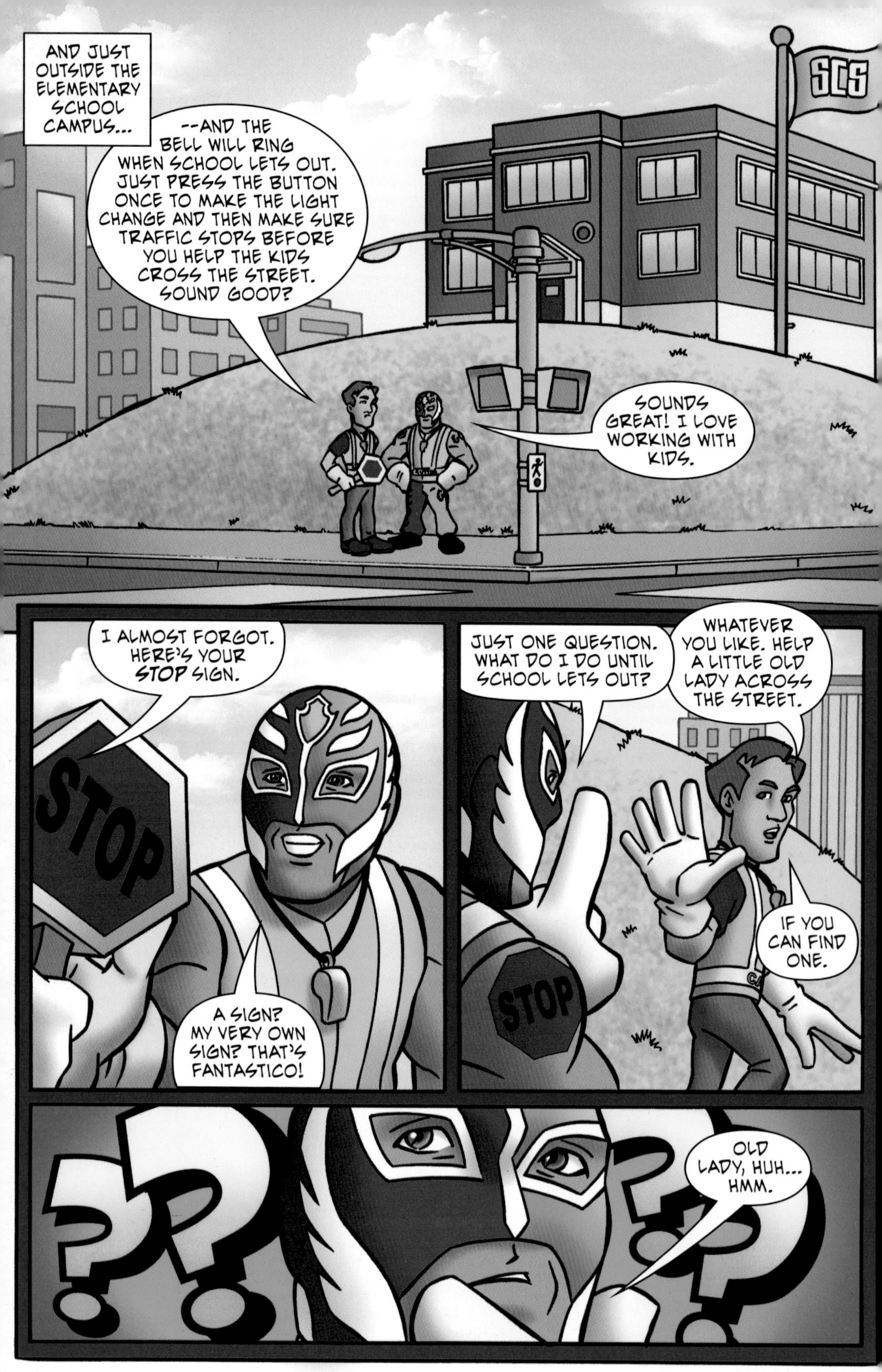
AND JUST OUTSIDE THE ELEMENTARY SCHOOL CAMPUS...
--AND THE BELL WILL RING WHEN SCHOOL LETS OUT. JUST PRESS THE BUTTON ONCE TO MAKE THE LIGHT CHANGE AND THEN MAKE SURE TRAFFIC STOPS BEFORE YOU HELP THE KIDS CROSS THE STREET. SOUND GOOD?
SOUNDS GREAT! I LOVE WORKING WITH KIDS.
SCS
I ALMOST FORGOT. HERE'S YOUR STOP SIGN.
STOP
A SIGN? MY VERY OWN SIGN? THAT'S FANTASTICO!
JUST ONE QUESTION. WHAT DO I DO UNTIL SCHOOL LETS OUT?
WHATEVER YOU LIKE. HELP A LITTLE OLD LADY ACROSS THE STREET.
IF YOU CAN FIND ONE.
STOP
OLD LADY, HUH... HMM.

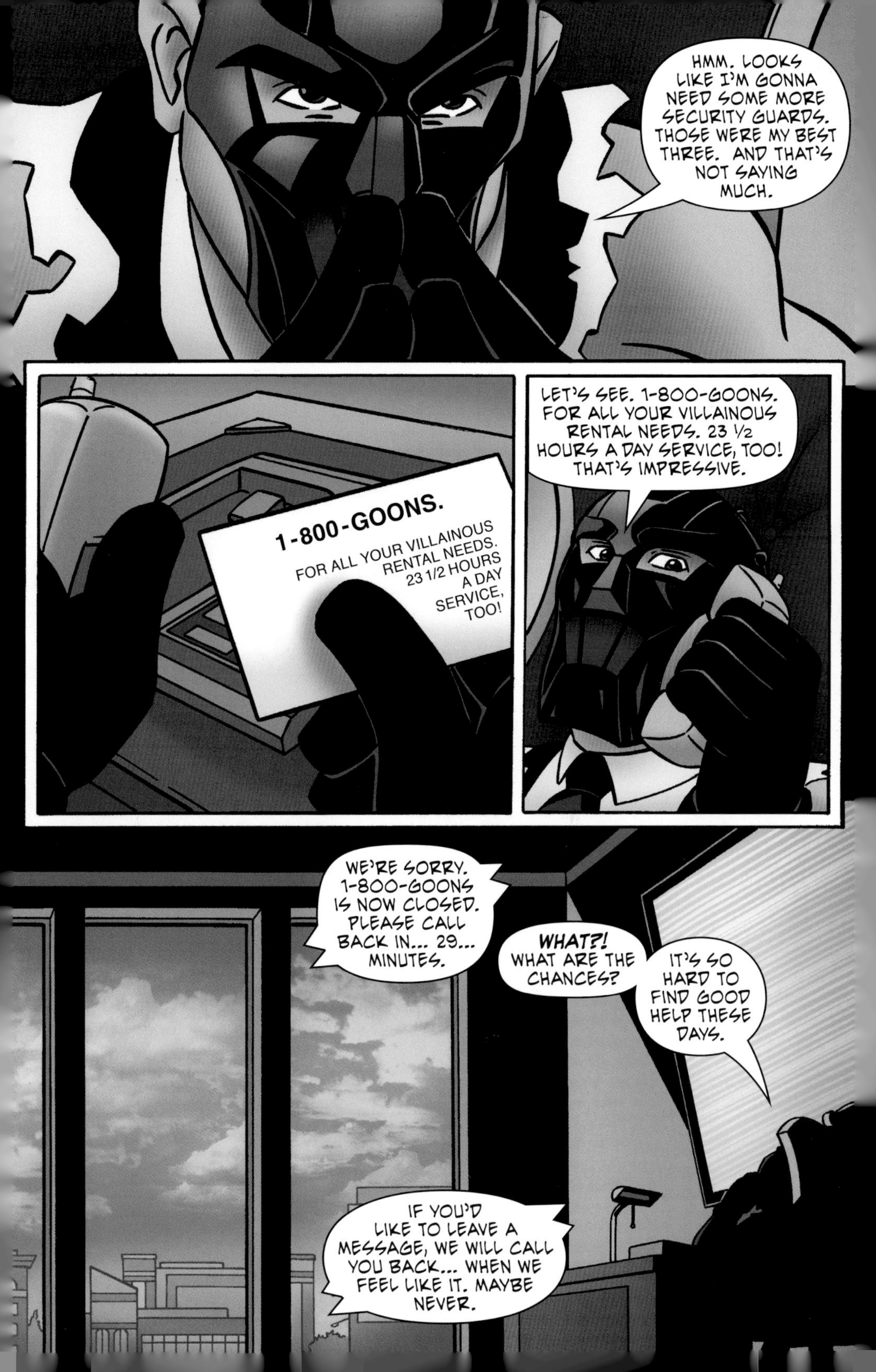
HMM. LOOKS LIKE I'M GONNA NEED SOME MORE SECURITY GUARDS. THOSE WERE MY BEST THREE. AND THAT'S NOT SAYING MUCH.
1-800-GOONS.
FOR ALL YOUR VILLAINOUS RENTAL NEEDS. 23 1/2 HOURS A DAY SERVICE, TOO!
LET'S SEE. 1-800-GOONS. FOR ALL YOUR VILLAINOUS RENTAL NEEDS. 23 ½ HOURS A DAY SERVICE, TOO! THAT'S IMPRESSIVE.
WE'RE SORRY. 1-800-GOONS IS NOW CLOSED. PLEASE CALL BACK IN... 29... MINUTES.
WHAT?! WHAT ARE THE CHANCES?
IT'S SO HARD TO FIND GOOD HELP THESE DAYS.
IF YOU'D LIKE TO LEAVE A MESSAGE, WE WILL CALL YOU BACK... WHEN WE FEEL LIKE IT. MAYBE NEVER.

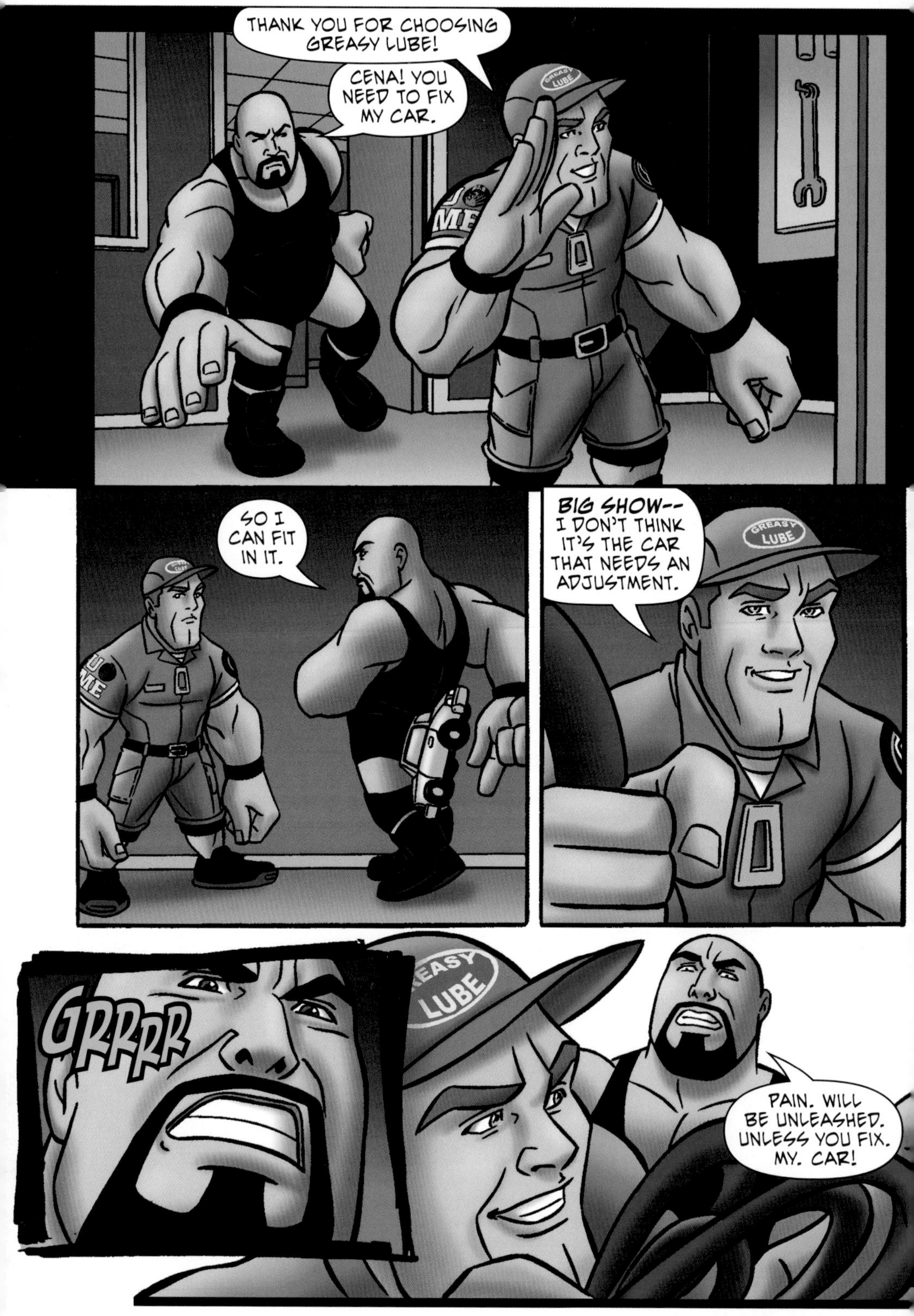
THANK YOU FOR CHOOSING GREASY LUBE!
CENA! YOU NEED TO FIX MY CAR.
GREASY LUBE
SO I CAN FIT IN IT.
BIG SHOW-- I DON'T THINK IT'S THE CAR THAT NEEDS AN ADJUSTMENT.
GREASY LUBE
GRRRR
PAIN. WILL BE UNLEASHED. UNLESS YOU FIX. MY. CAR!

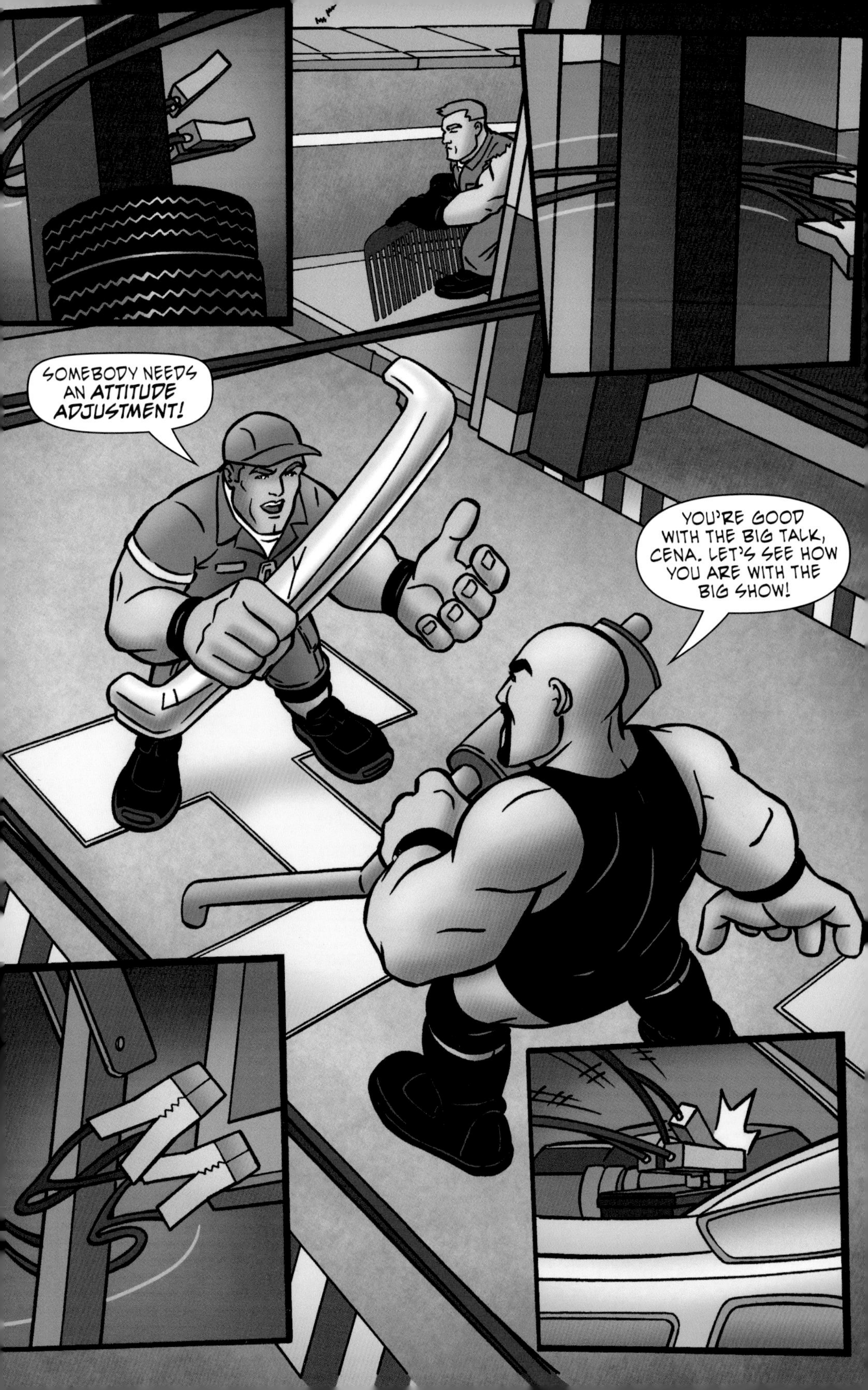
SOMEBODY NEEDS AN ATTITUDE ADJUSTMENT!
YOU'RE GOOD WITH THE BIG TALK, CENA. LET'S SEE HOW YOU ARE WITH THE BIG SHOW!

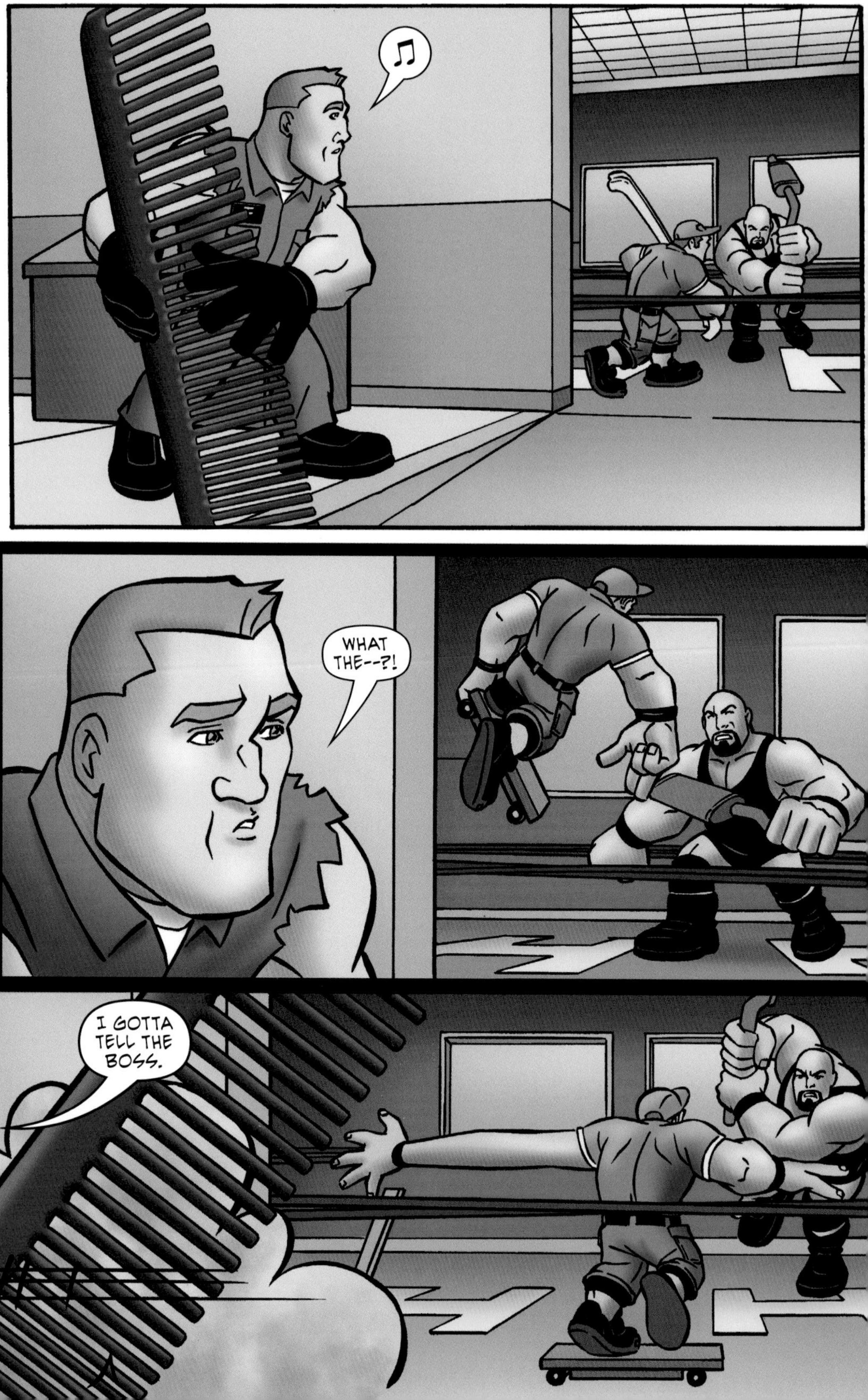
♫
WHAT THE--?!
I GOTTA TELL THE BOSS.

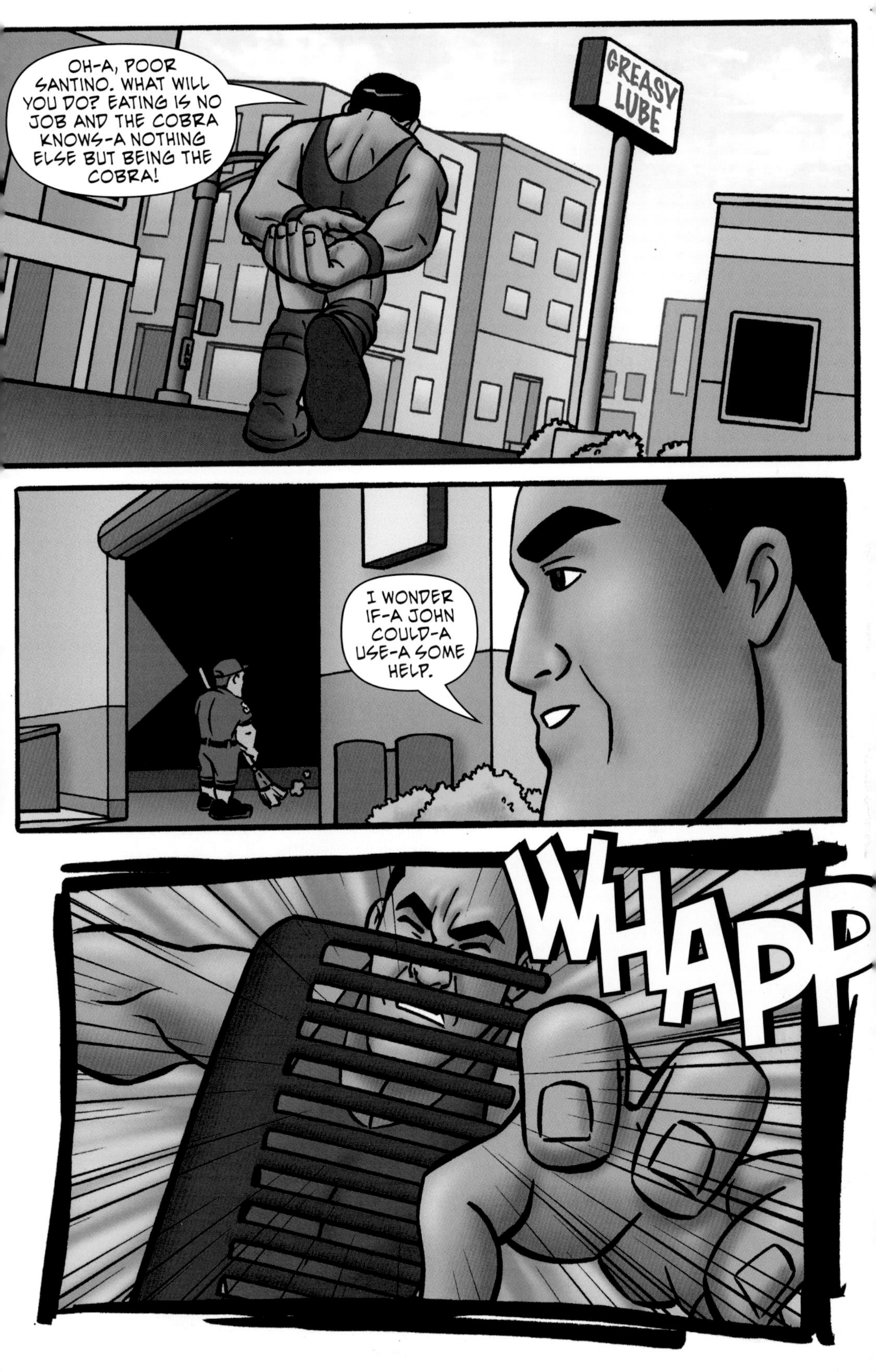
OH-A, POOR SANTINO. WHAT WILL YOU DO? EATING IS NO JOB AND THE COBRA KNOWS-A NOTHING ELSE BUT BEING THE COBRA!
GREASY LUBE
I WONDER IF-A JOHN COULD-A USE-A SOME HELP.
WHAPP

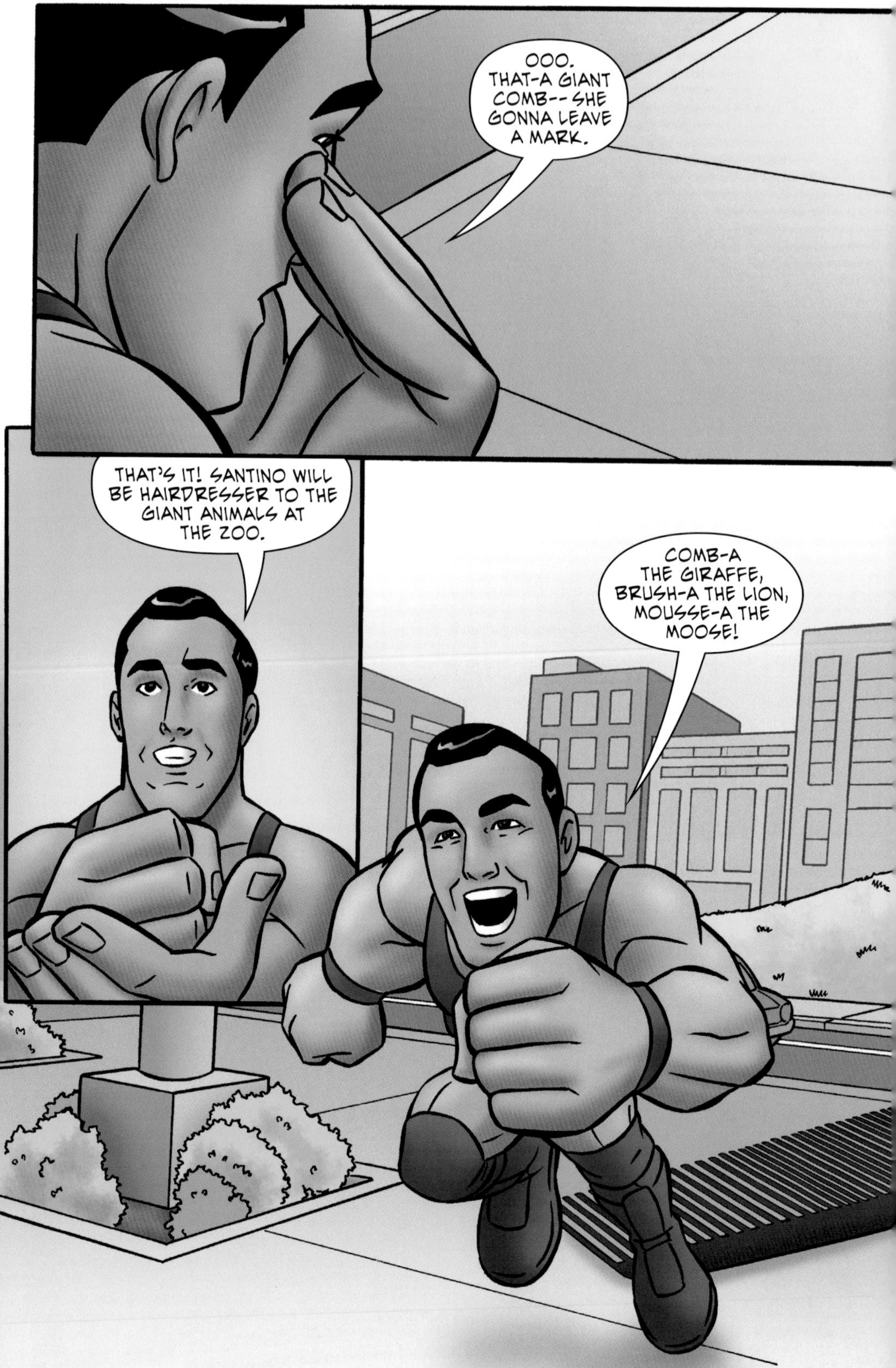
OOO. THAT-A GIANT COMB-- SHE GONNA LEAVE A MARK.
THAT'S IT! SANTINO WILL BE HAIRDRESSER TO THE GIANT ANIMALS AT THE ZOO.
COMB-A THE GIRAFFE, BRUSH-A THE LION, MOUSSE-A THE MOOSE!

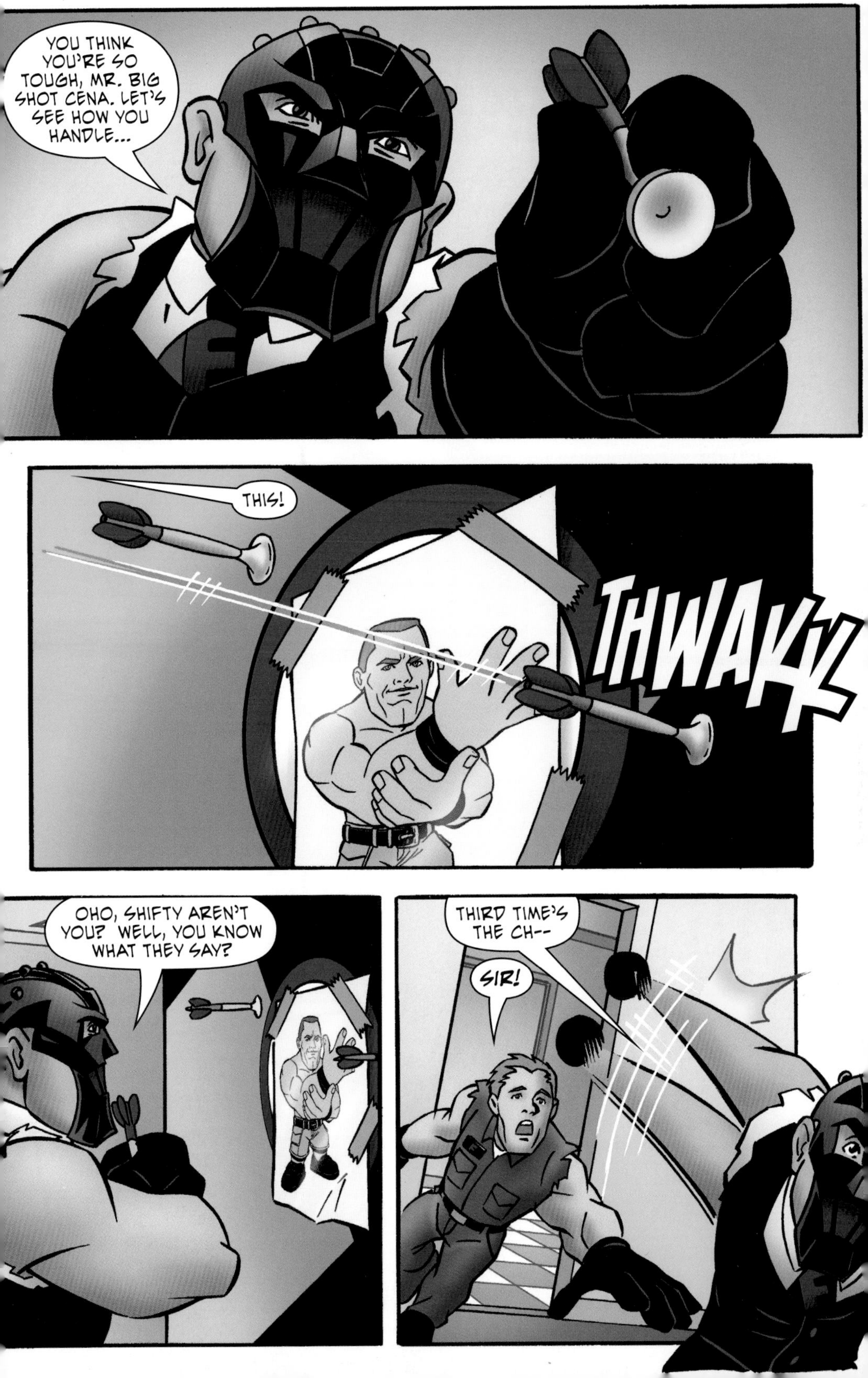
YOU THINK YOU'RE SO TOUGH, MR. BIG SHOT CENA. LET'S SEE HOW YOU HANDLE...
THIS!
THWAKK!
OHO, SHIFTY AREN'T YOU? WELL, YOU KNOW WHAT THEY SAY?
THIRD TIME'S THE CH--
SIR!

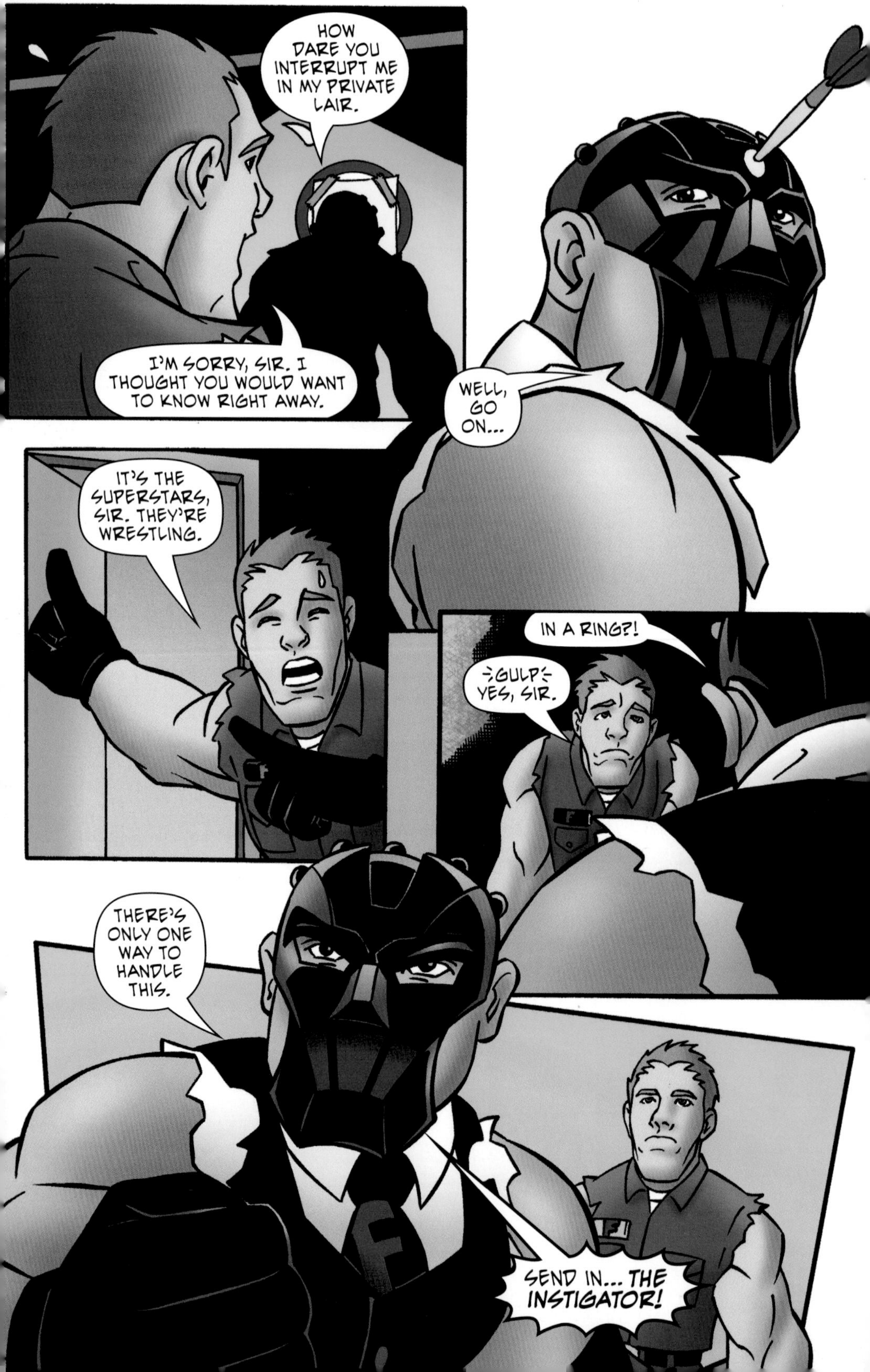
HOW DARE YOU INTERRUPT ME IN MY PRIVATE LAIR.
I'M SORRY, SIR. I THOUGHT YOU WOULD WANT TO KNOW RIGHT AWAY.
WELL, GO ON...
IT'S THE SUPERSTARS, SIR. THEY'RE WRESTLING.
IN A RING?!
GULP
YES, SIR.
THERE'S ONLY ONE WAY TO HANDLE THIS.
SEND IN... THE INSTIGATOR!

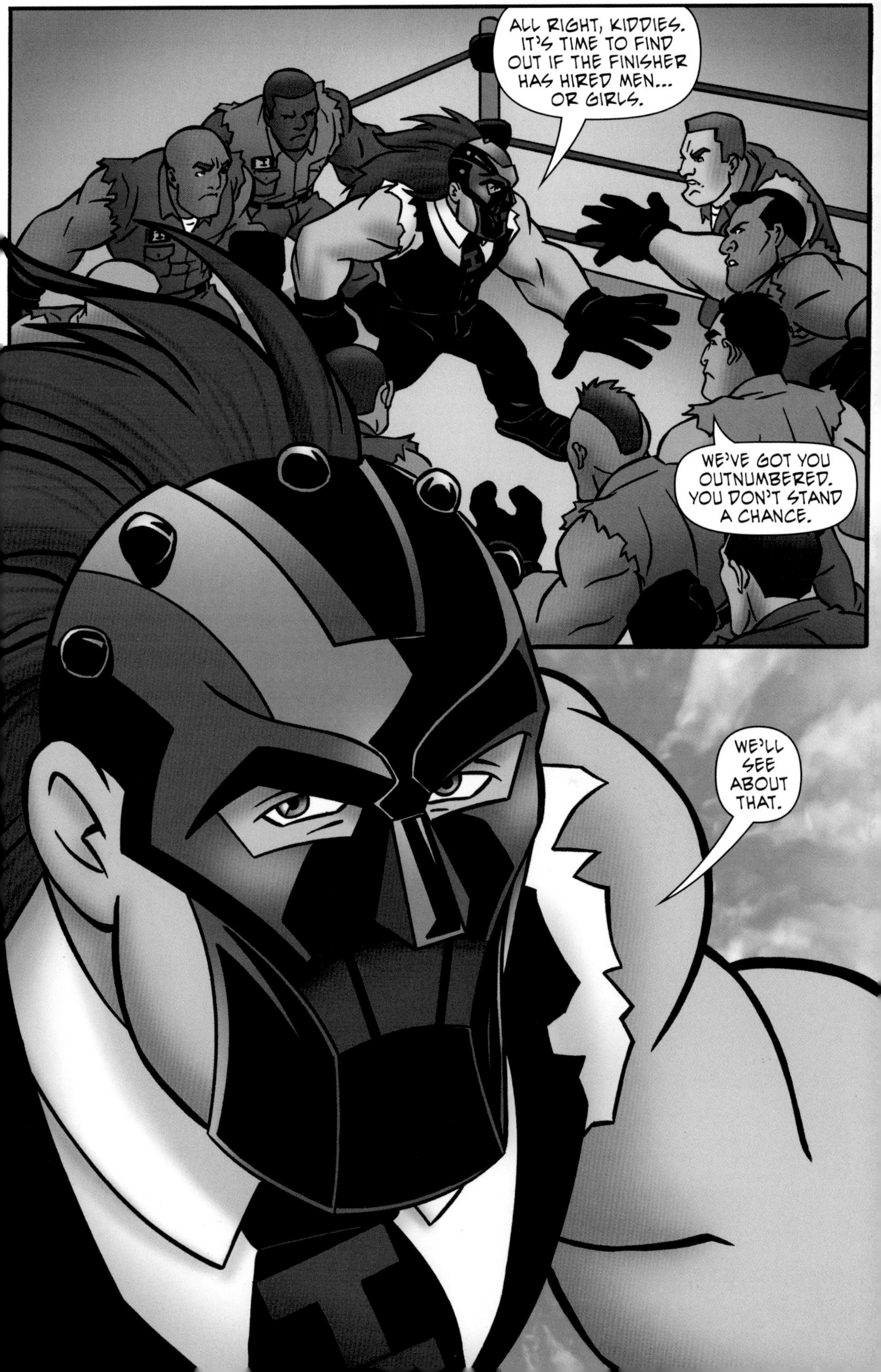
ALL RIGHT, KIDDIES. IT'S TIME TO FIND OUT IF THE FINISHER HAS HIRED MEN... OR GIRLS.
WE'VE GOT YOU OUTNUMBERED. YOU DON'T STAND A CHANCE.
WE'LL SEE ABOUT THAT.

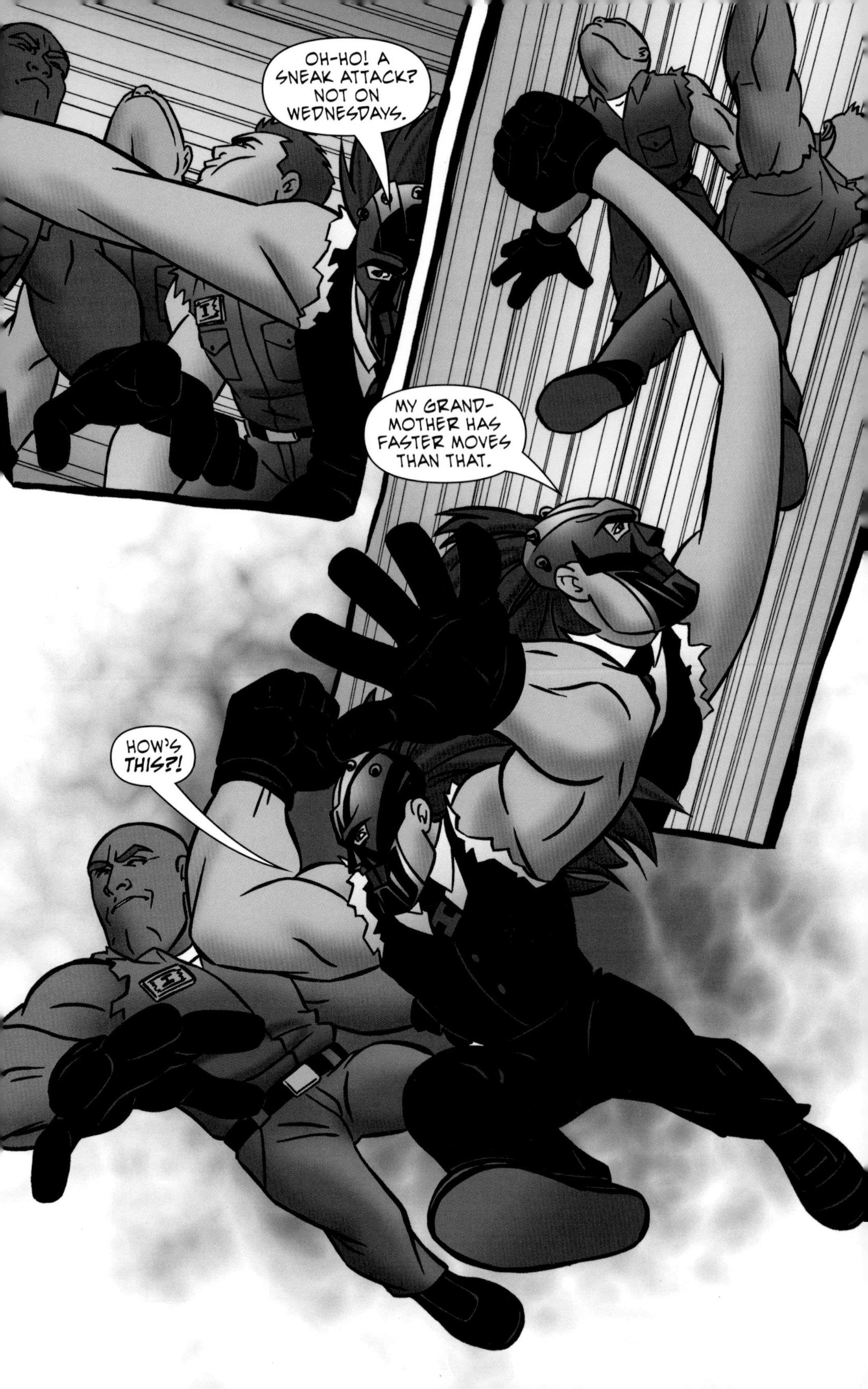
OH-HO! A SNEAK ATTACK? NOT ON WEDNESDAYS.
MY GRAND-MOTHER HAS FASTER MOVES THAN THAT.
HOW'S THIS?!

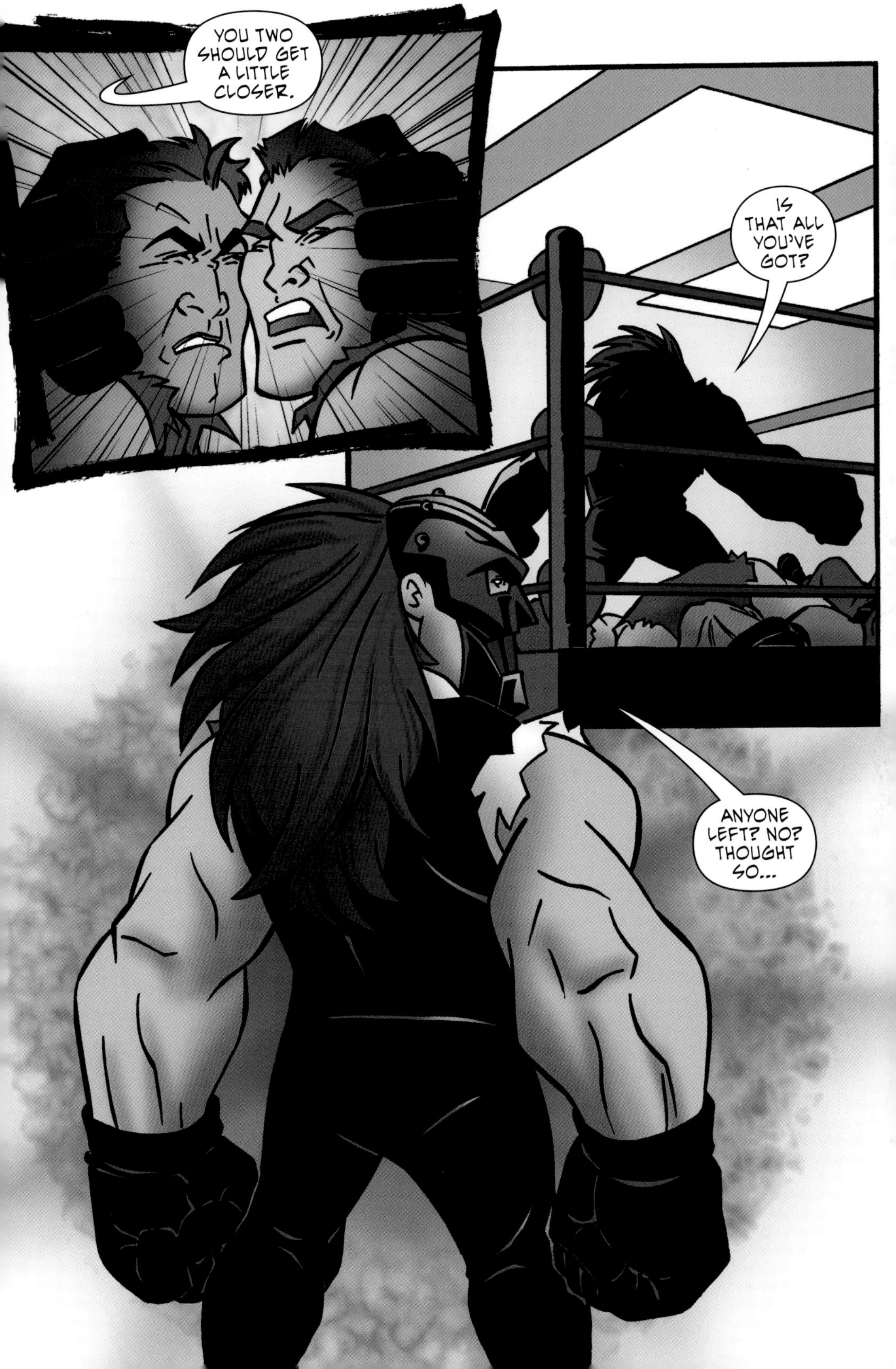
YOU TWO SHOULD GET A LITTLE CLOSER.
IS THAT ALL YOU'VE GOT?
ANYONE LEFT? NO? THOUGHT SO...

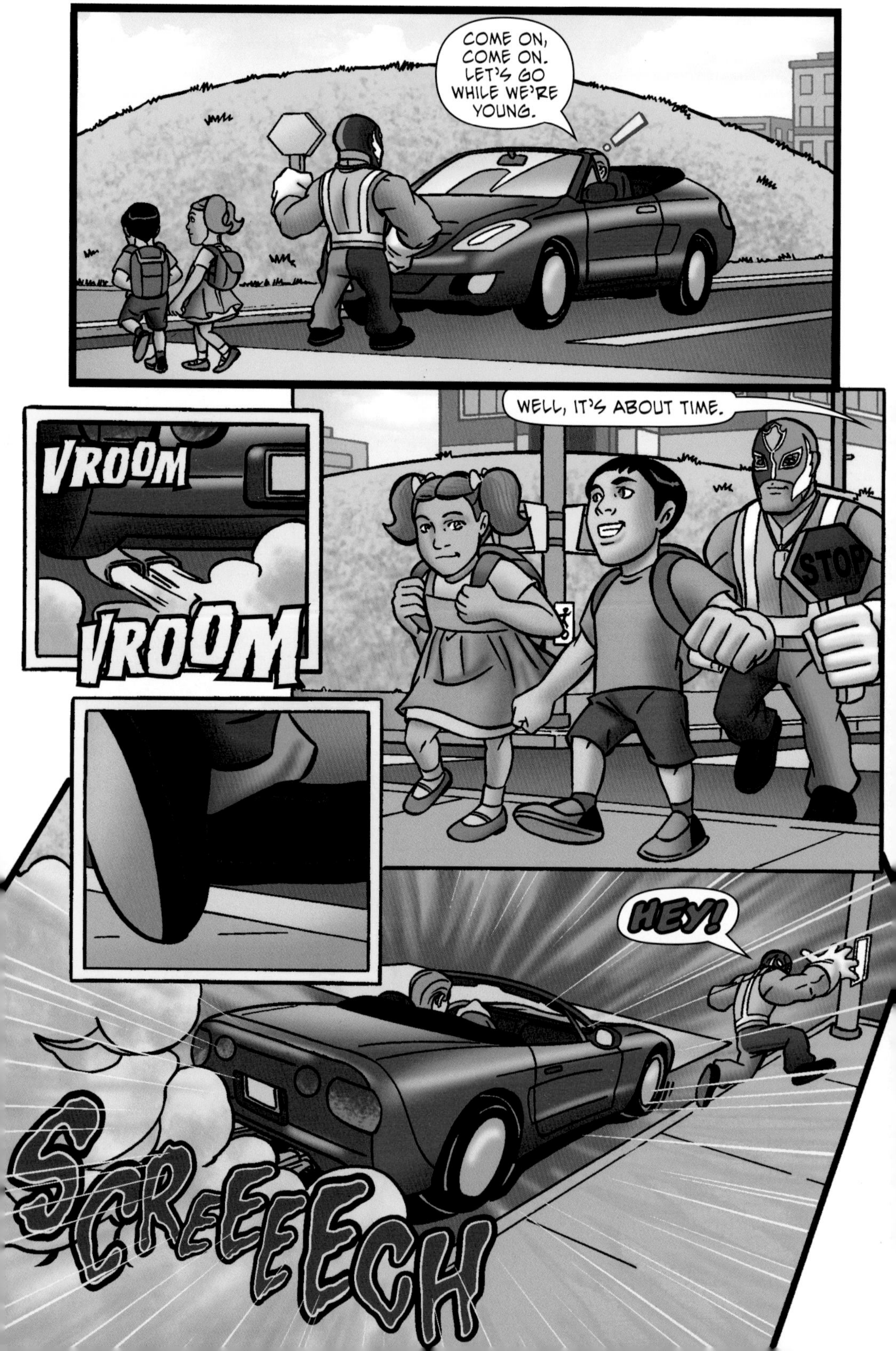
COME ON, COME ON. LET'S GO WHILE WE'RE YOUNG.
!
WELL, IT'S ABOUT TIME.
STOP
VROOM
VROOM
HEY!
SCREEEECH

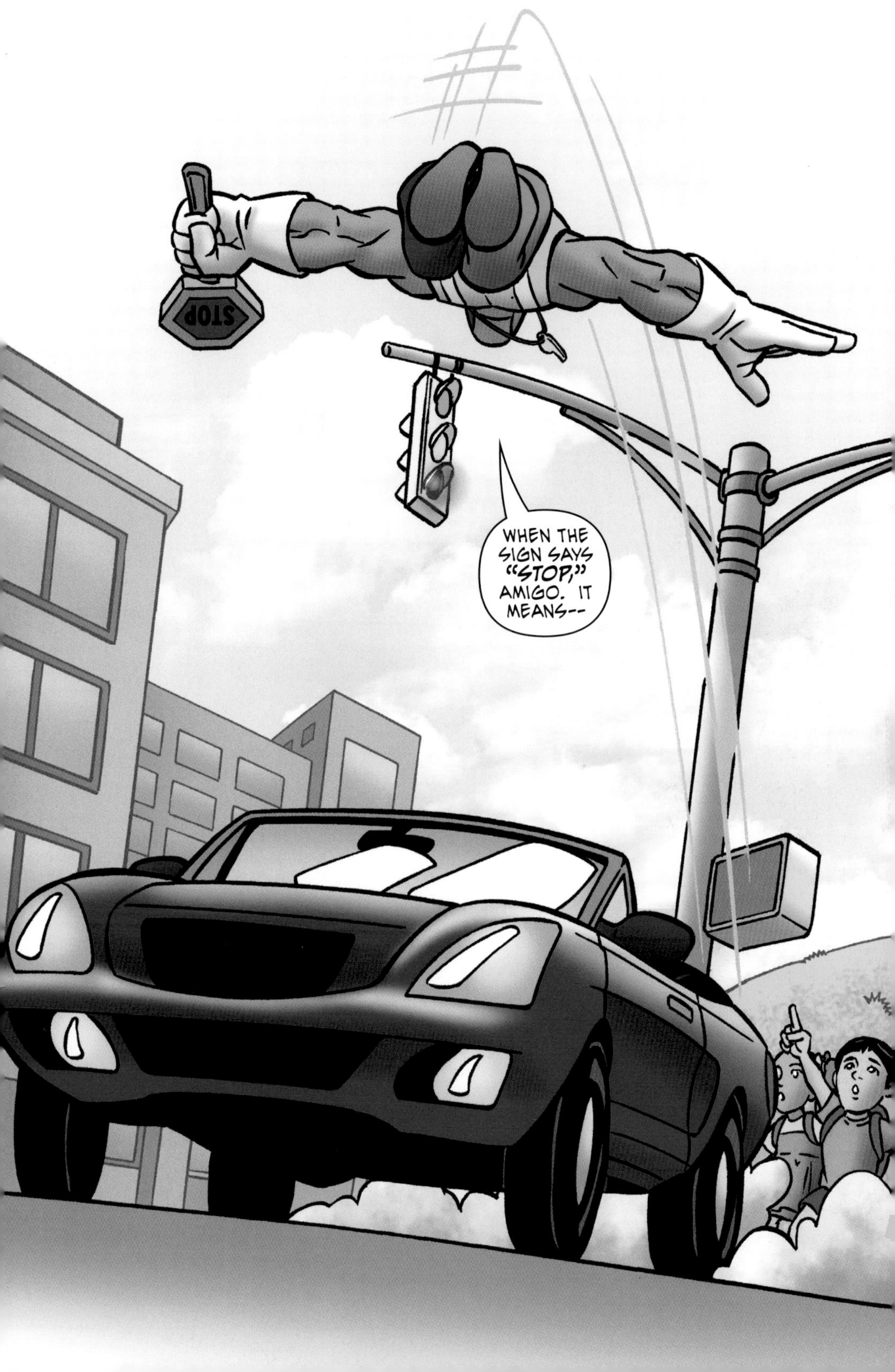
STOP
WHEN THE SIGN SAYS "STOP," AMIGO. IT MEANS--

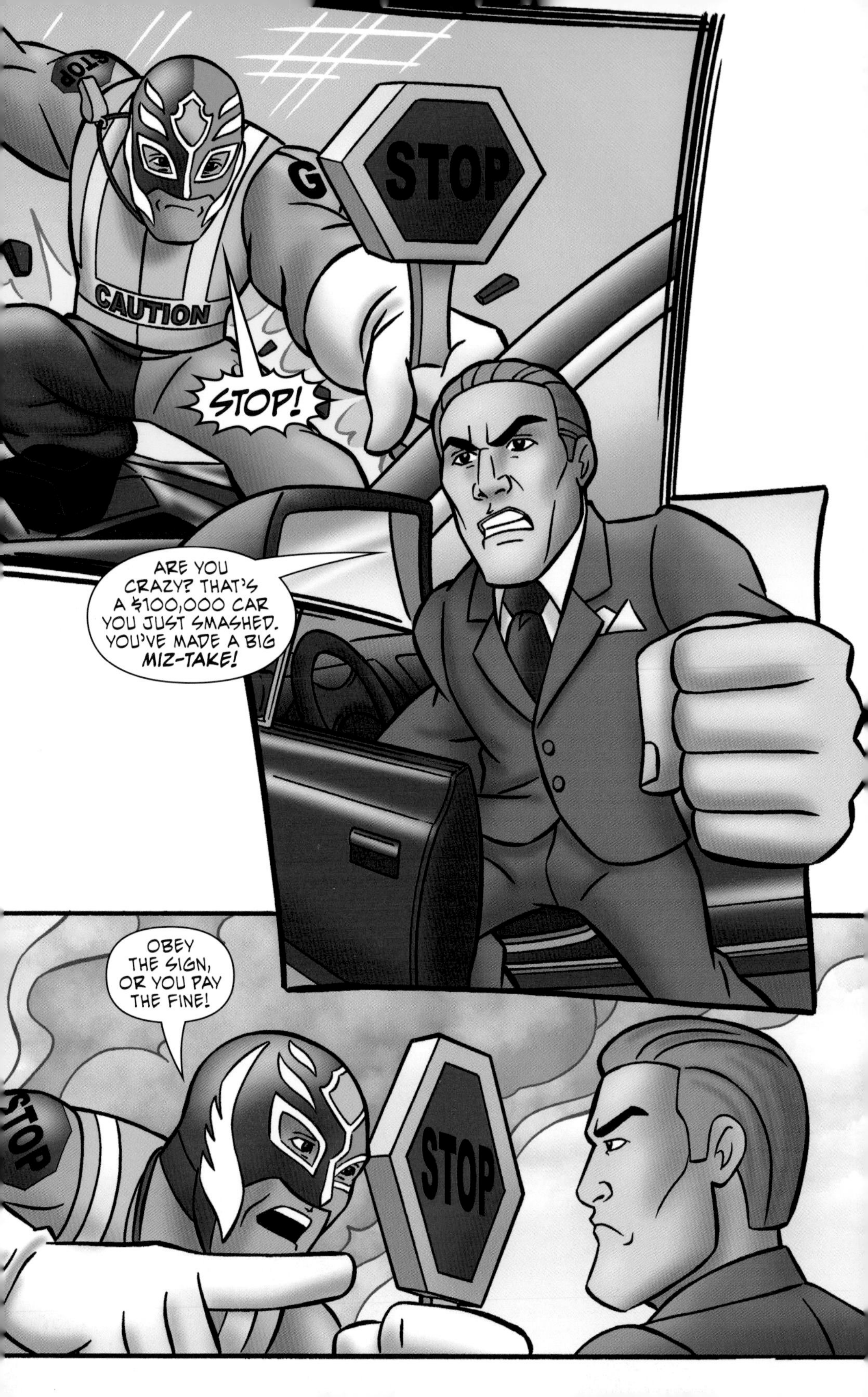
STOP
CAUTION
STOP!
ARE YOU CRAZY? THAT'S A $100,000 CAR YOU JUST SMASHED. YOU'VE MADE A BIG MIZ-TAKE!
OBEY THE SIGN, OR YOU PAY THE FINE!
STOP

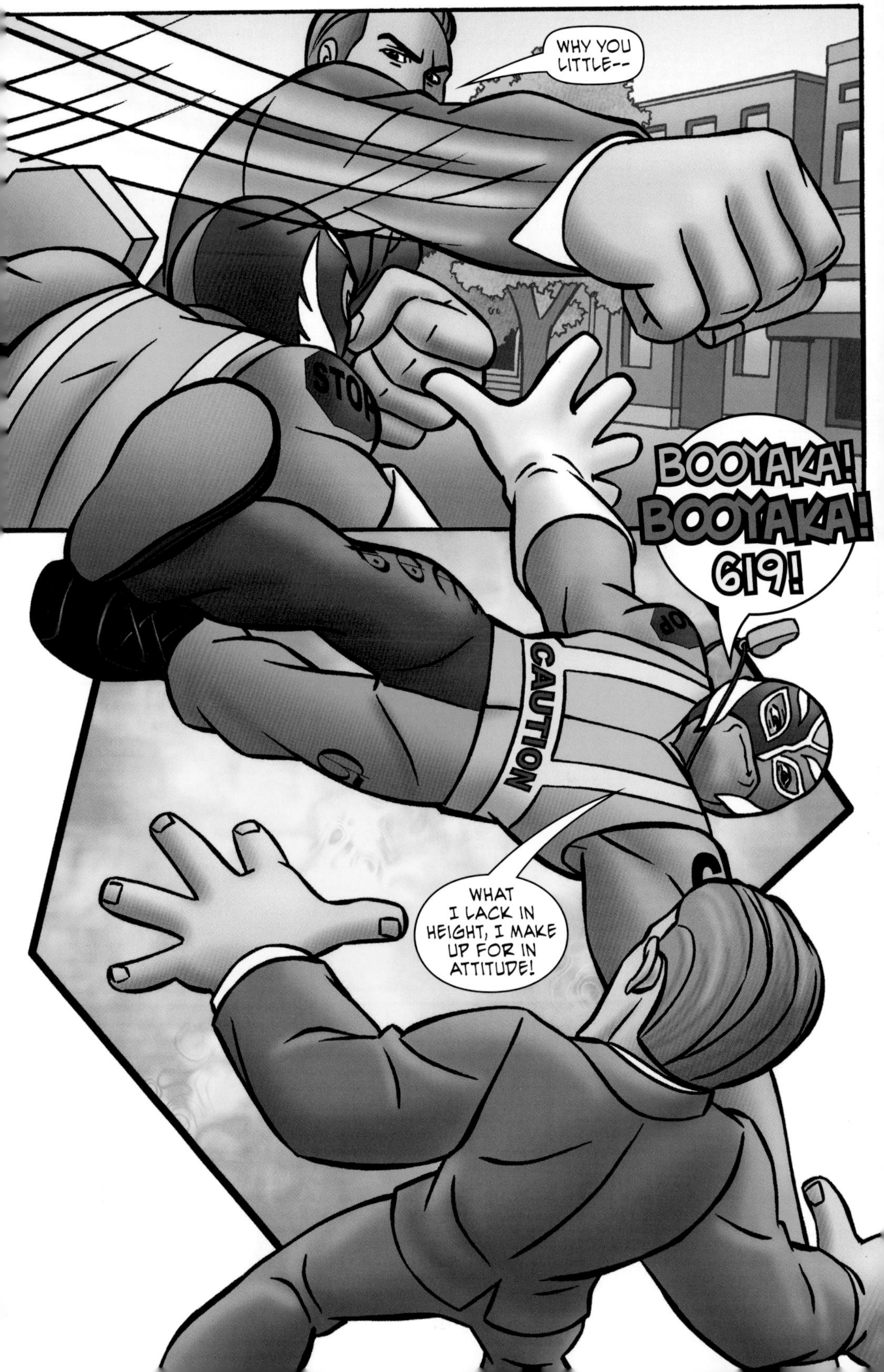

WHY YOU LITTLE--
BOOYAKA! BOOYAKA! 619!
WHAT I LACK IN HEIGHT, I MAKE UP FOR IN ATTITUDE!

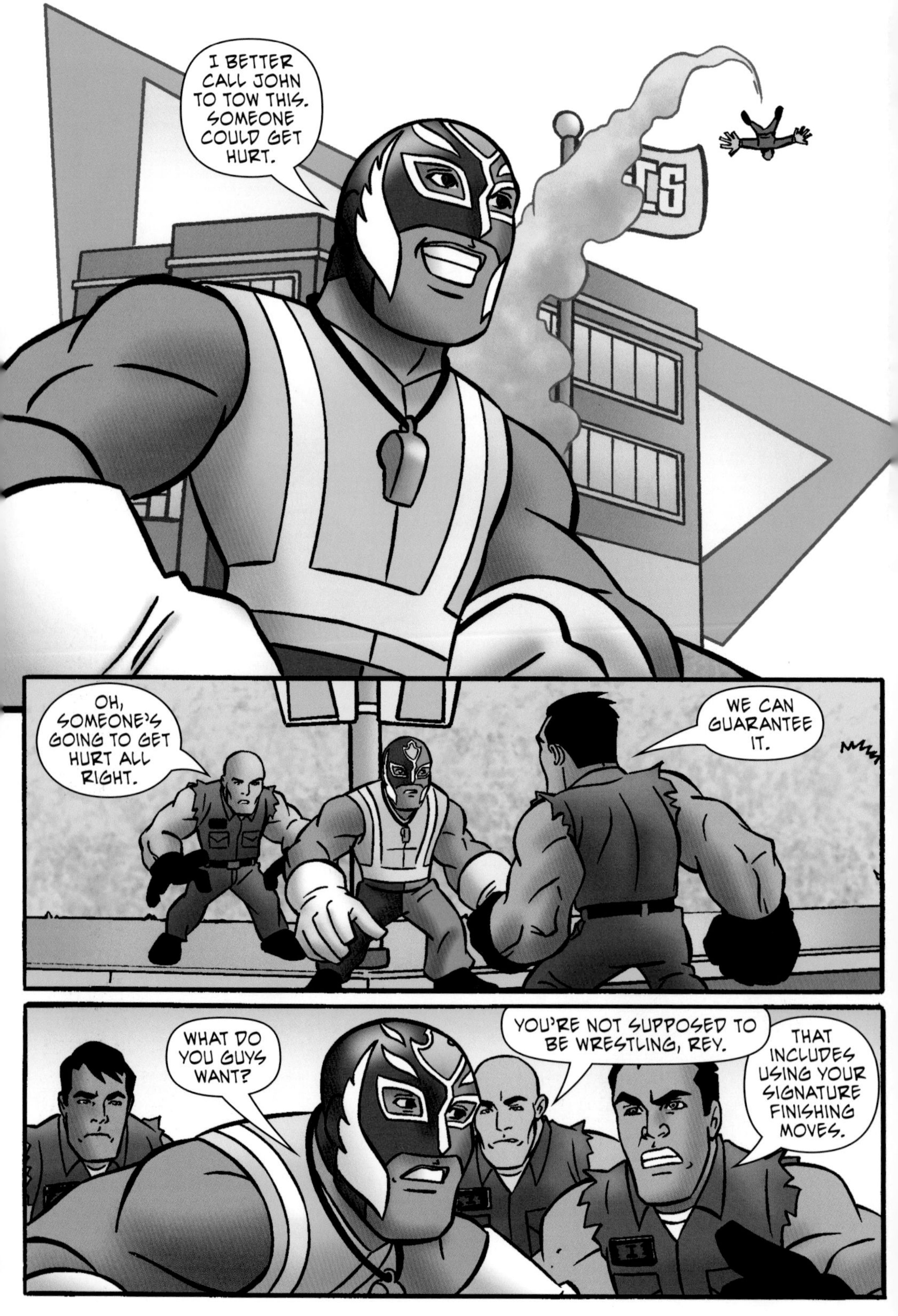

I BETTER CALL JOHN TO TOW THIS. SOMEONE COULD GET HURT.
OH, SOMEONE'S GOING TO GET HURT ALL RIGHT.
WE CAN GUARANTEE IT.
WHAT DO YOU GUYS WANT?
YOU'RE NOT SUPPOSED TO BE WRESTLING, REY.
THAT INCLUDES USING YOUR SIGNATURE FINISHING MOVES.

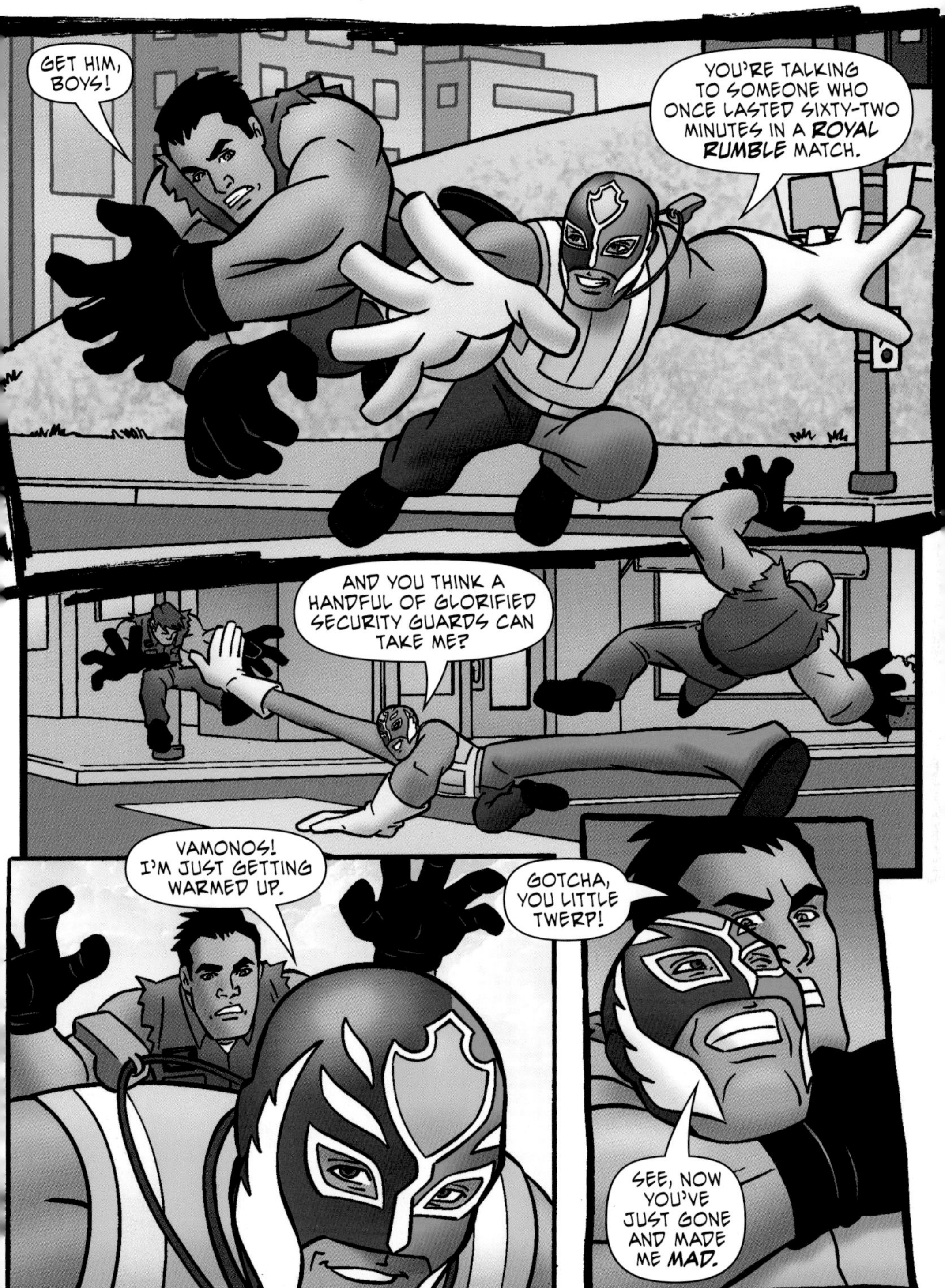
GET HIM, BOYS!
YOU'RE TALKING TO SOMEONE WHO ONCE LASTED SIXTY-TWO MINUTES IN A ROYAL RUMBLE MATCH.
AND YOU THINK A HANDFUL OF GLORIFIED SECURITY GUARDS CAN TAKE ME?
VAMONOS! I'M JUST GETTING WARMED UP.
GOTCHA, YOU LITTLE TWERP!
SEE, NOW YOU'VE JUST GONE AND MADE ME MAD.

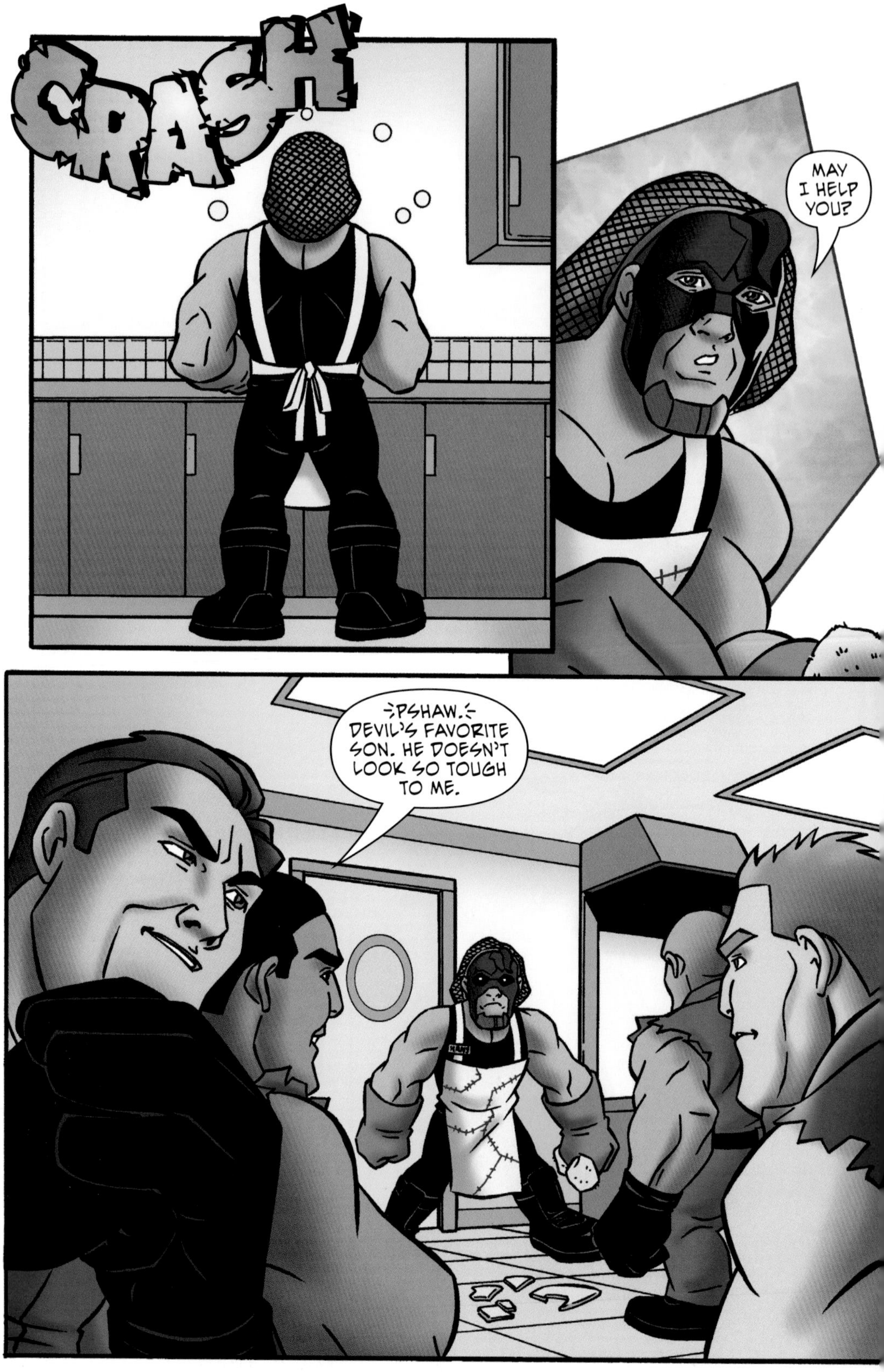
CRASH
MAY I HELP YOU?
PSHAW. DEVIL'S FAVORITE SON. HE DOESN'T LOOK SO TOUGH TO ME.

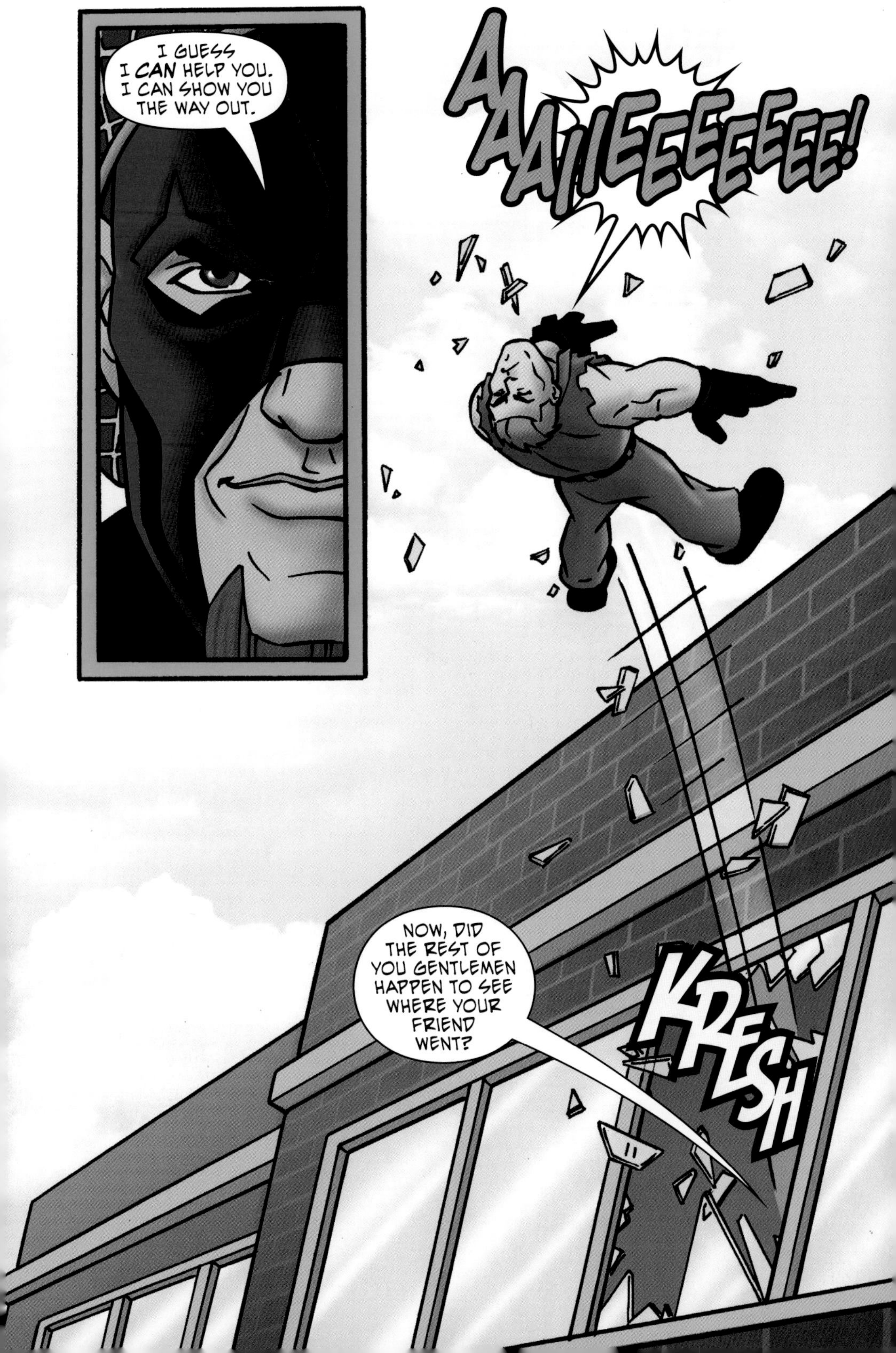
I GUESS I CAN HELP YOU. I CAN SHOW YOU THE WAY OUT.
AAAIIEEEEEEEE!
NOW, DID THE REST OF YOU GENTLEMEN HAPPEN TO SEE WHERE YOUR FRIEND WENT?
KRESH

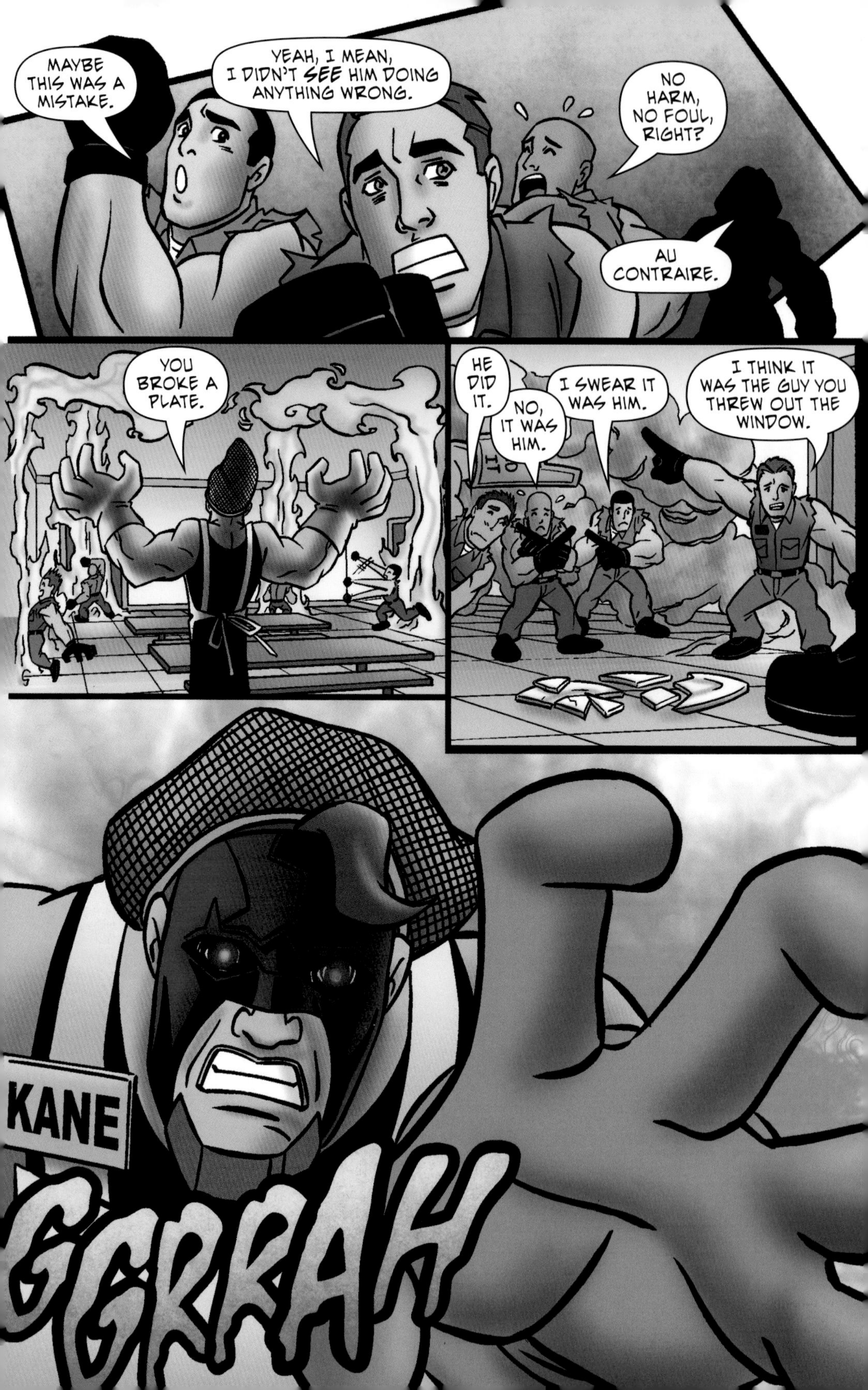
MAYBE THIS WAS A MISTAKE.
YEAH, I MEAN, I DIDN'T SEE HIM DOING ANYTHING WRONG.
NO HARM, NO FOUL, RIGHT?
AU CONTRAIRE.
YOU BROKE A PLATE.
HE DID IT.
NO, IT WAS HIM.
I SWEAR IT WAS HIM.
I THINK IT WAS THE GUY YOU THREW OUT THE WINDOW.
KANE
GGRRAH

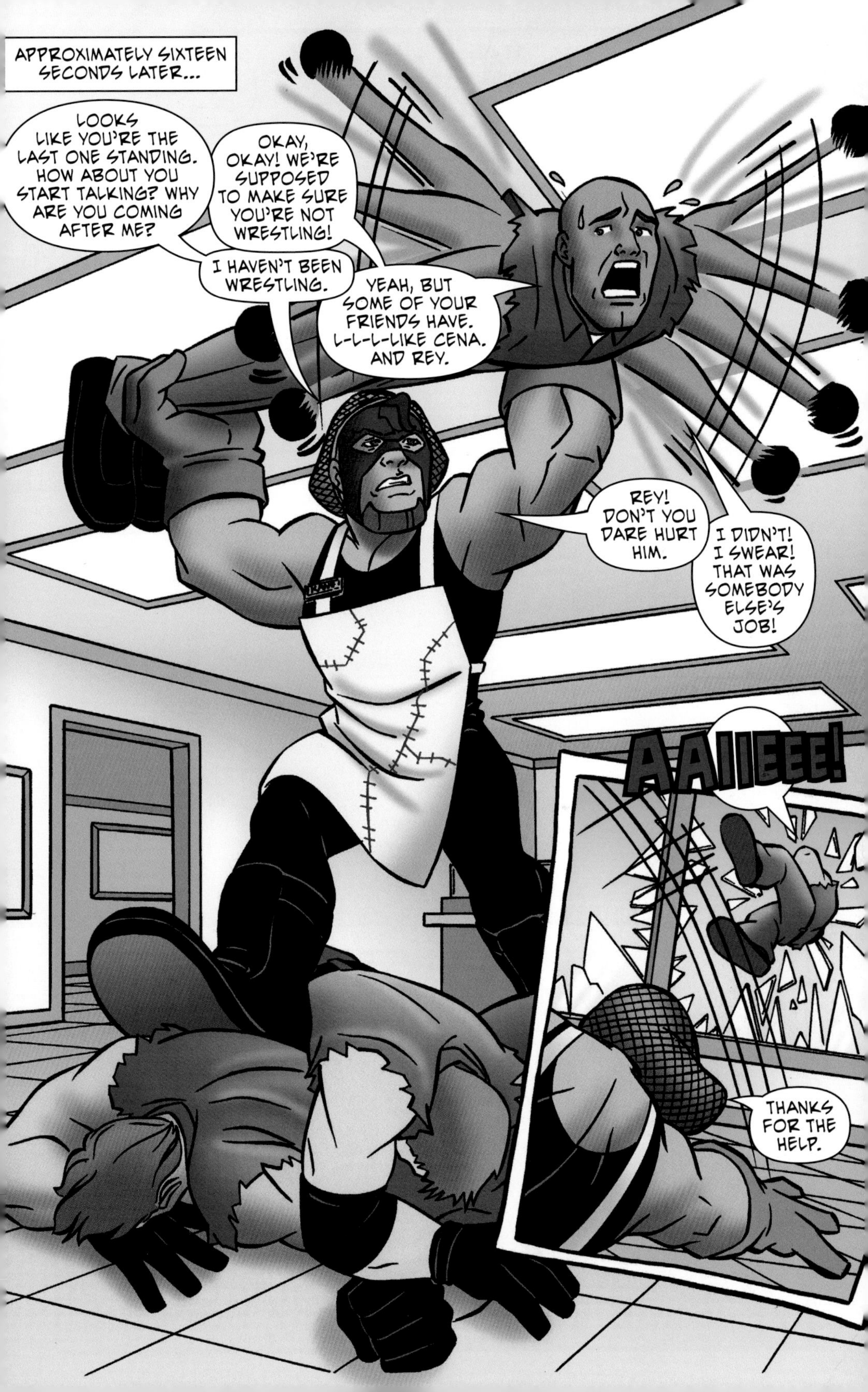
APPROXIMATELY SIXTEEN SECONDS LATER...
LOOKS LIKE YOU'RE THE LAST ONE STANDING. HOW ABOUT YOU START TALKING? WHY ARE YOU COMING AFTER ME?
OKAY, OKAY! WE'RE SUPPOSED TO MAKE SURE YOU'RE NOT WRESTLING!
I HAVEN'T BEEN WRESTLING.
YEAH, BUT SOME OF YOUR FRIENDS HAVE. L-L-L-LIKE CENA. AND REY.
REY! DON'T YOU DARE HURT HIM.
I DIDN'T! I SWEAR! THAT WAS SOMEBODY ELSE'S JOB!
AAIIEEE!
THANKS FOR THE HELP.

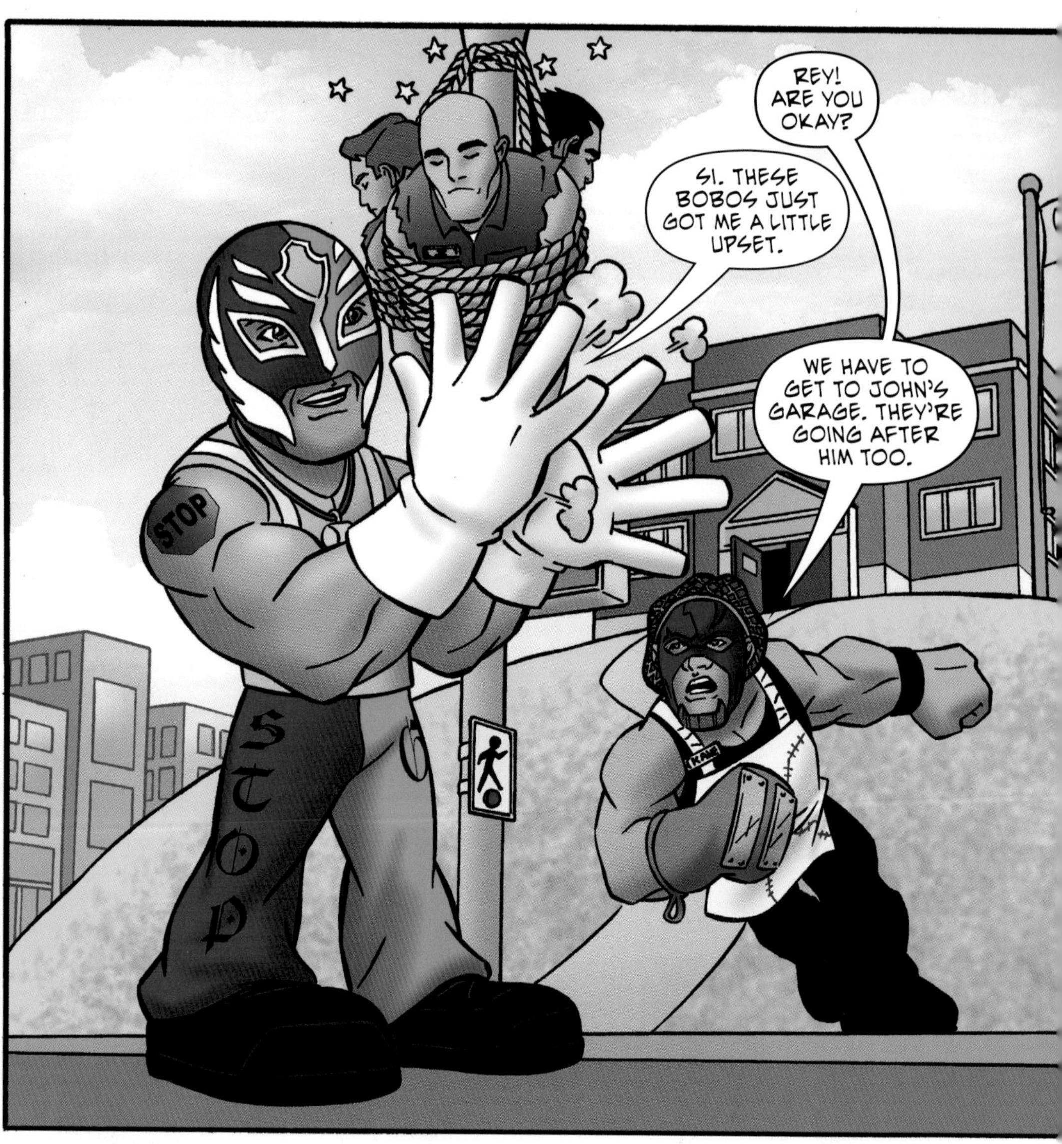
REY! ARE YOU OKAY?
SI. THESE BOBOS JUST GOT ME A LITTLE UPSET.
WE HAVE TO GET TO JOHN'S GARAGE. THEY'RE GOING AFTER HIM TOO.
STOP
STOP

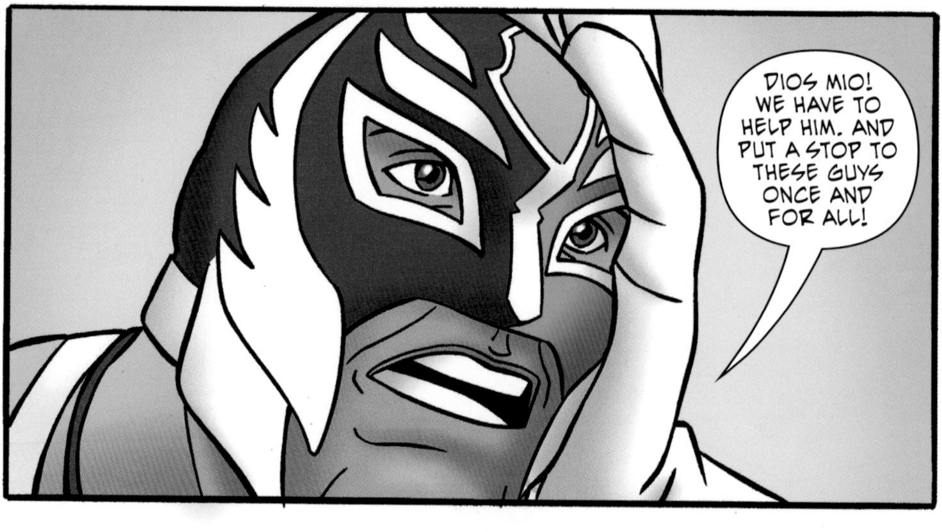
DIOS MIO! WE HAVE TO HELP HIM. AND PUT A STOP TO THESE GUYS ONCE AND FOR ALL!

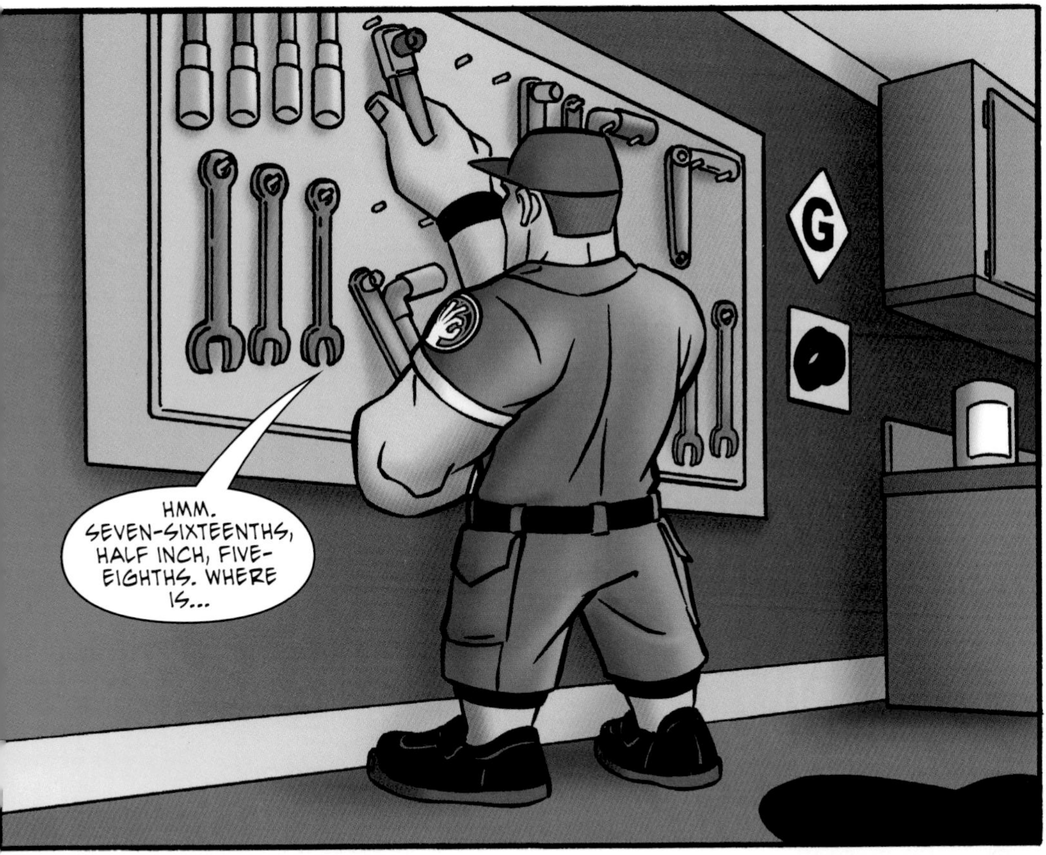
HMM. SEVEN-SIXTEENTHS, HALF INCH, FIVE-EIGHTHS. WHERE IS...
G

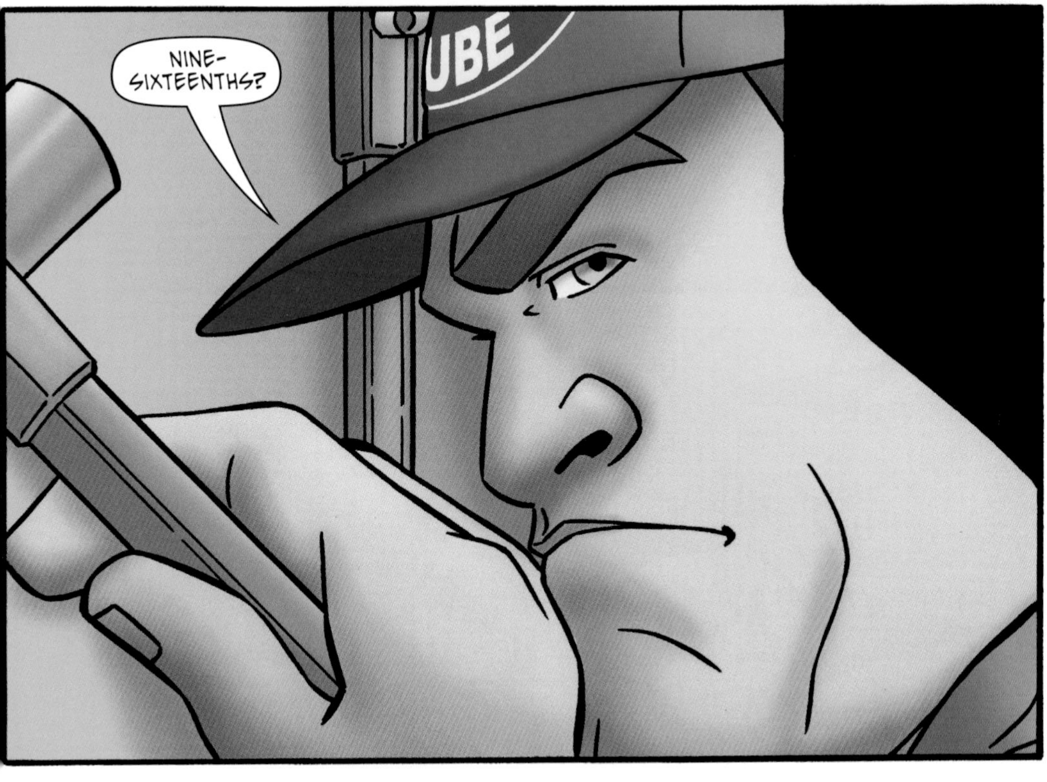
NINE-SIXTEENTHS?
UBE

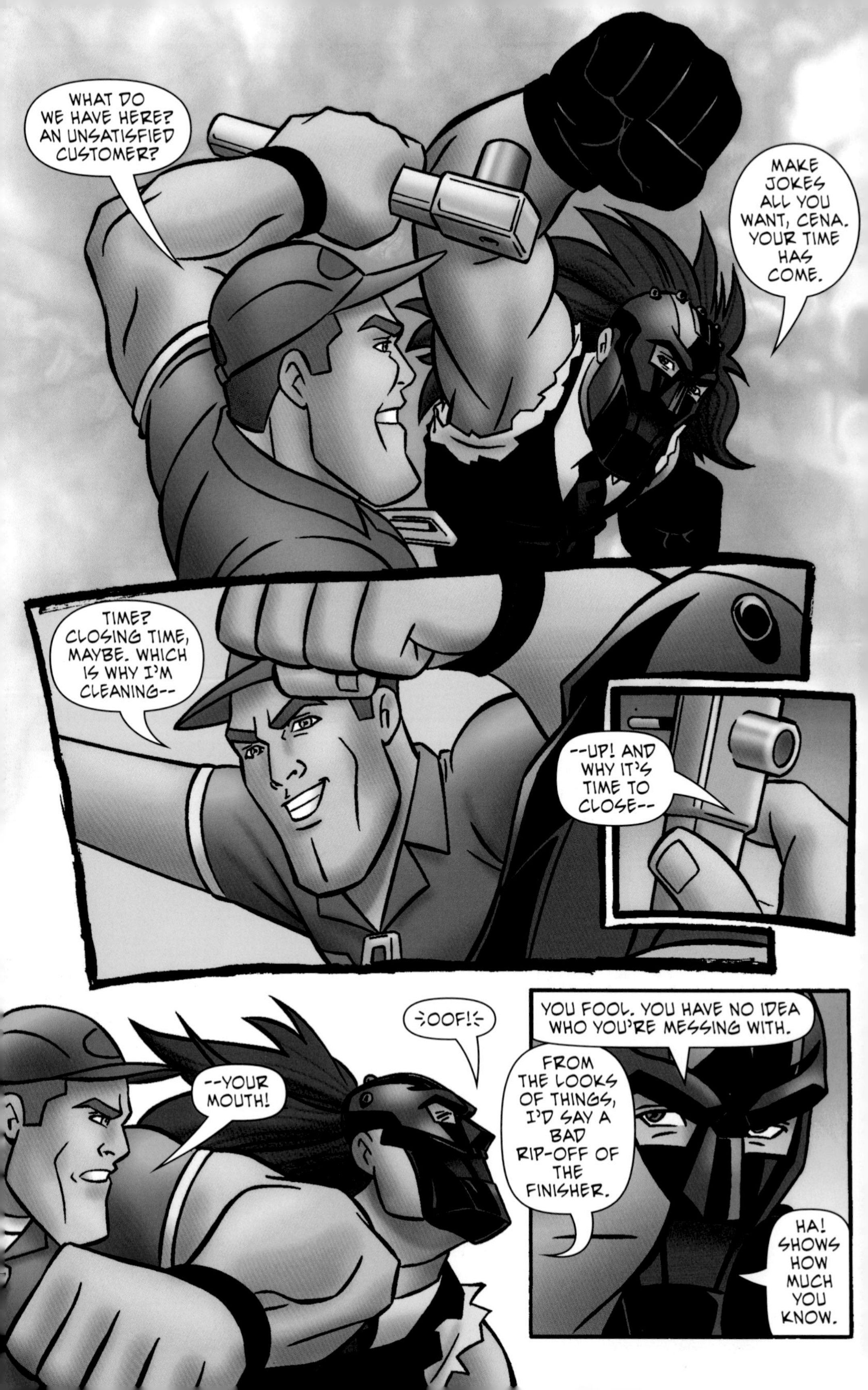
WHAT DO WE HAVE HERE? AN UNSATISFIED CUSTOMER?
MAKE JOKES ALL YOU WANT, CENA. YOUR TIME HAS COME.
TIME? CLOSING TIME, MAYBE. WHICH IS WHY I'M CLEANING--
--UP! AND WHY IT'S TIME TO CLOSE--
--YOUR MOUTH!
OOF!
YOU FOOL. YOU HAVE NO IDEA WHO YOU'RE MESSING WITH.
FROM THE LOOKS OF THINGS, I'D SAY A BAD RIP-OFF OF THE FINISHER.
HA! SHOWS HOW MUCH YOU KNOW.

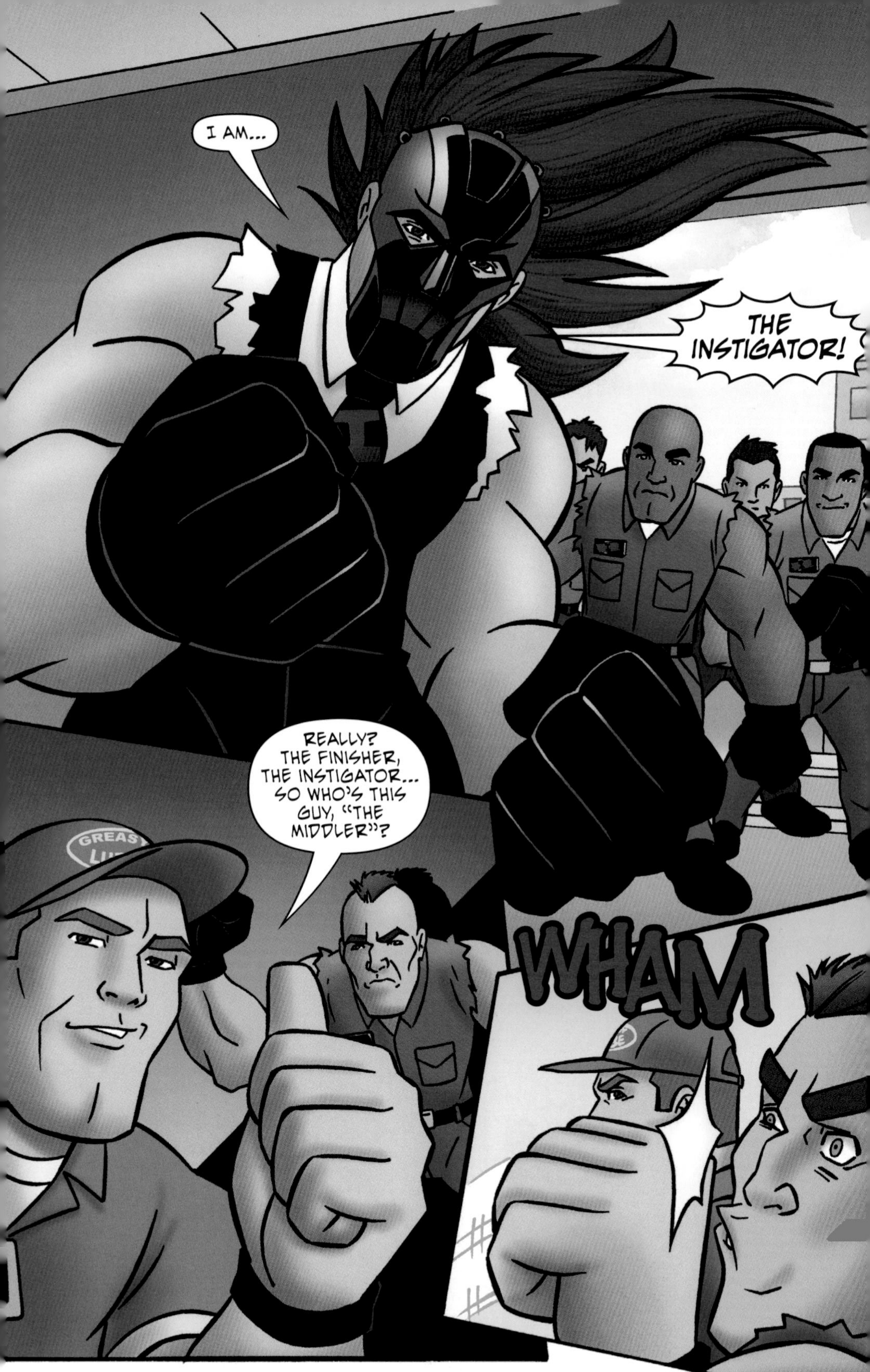
I AM...
THE INSTIGATOR!
REALLY? THE FINISHER, THE INSTIGATOR... SO WHO'S THIS GUY, "THE MIDDLER"?
WHAM

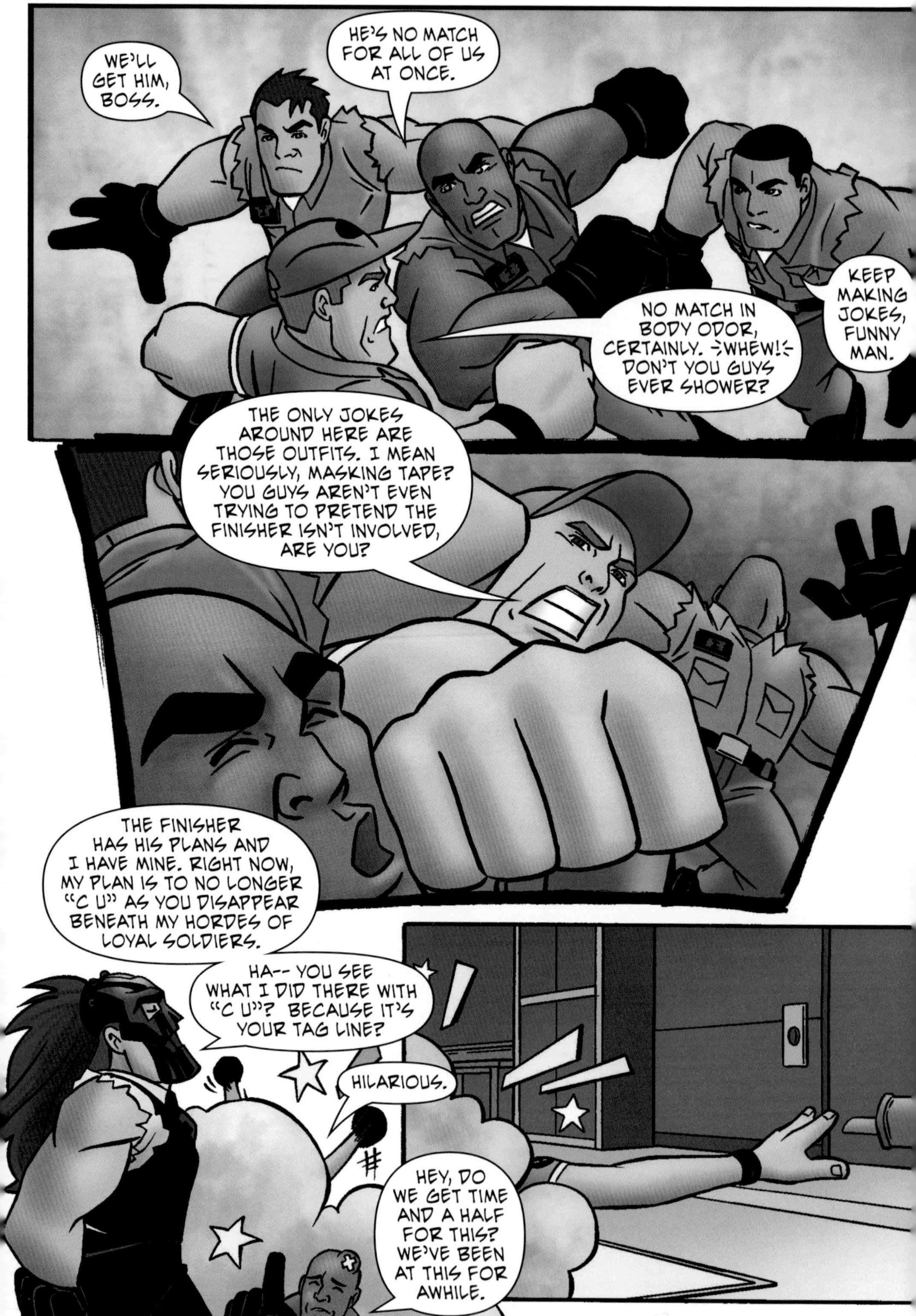
WE'LL GET HIM, BOSS.
HE'S NO MATCH FOR ALL OF US AT ONCE.
NO MATCH IN BODY ODOR, CERTAINLY. *WHEW!* DON'T YOU GUYS EVER SHOWER?
KEEP MAKING JOKES, FUNNY MAN.
THE ONLY JOKES AROUND HERE ARE THOSE OUTFITS. I MEAN SERIOUSLY, MASKING TAPE? YOU GUYS AREN'T EVEN TRYING TO PRETEND THE FINISHER ISN'T INVOLVED, ARE YOU?
THE FINISHER HAS HIS PLANS AND I HAVE MINE. RIGHT NOW, MY PLAN IS TO NO LONGER "C U" AS YOU DISAPPEAR BENEATH MY HORDES OF LOYAL SOLDIERS.
HA-- YOU SEE WHAT I DID THERE WITH "C U"? BECAUSE IT'S YOUR TAG LINE?
HILARIOUS.
HEY, DO WE GET TIME AND A HALF FOR THIS? WE'VE BEEN AT THIS FOR AWHILE.

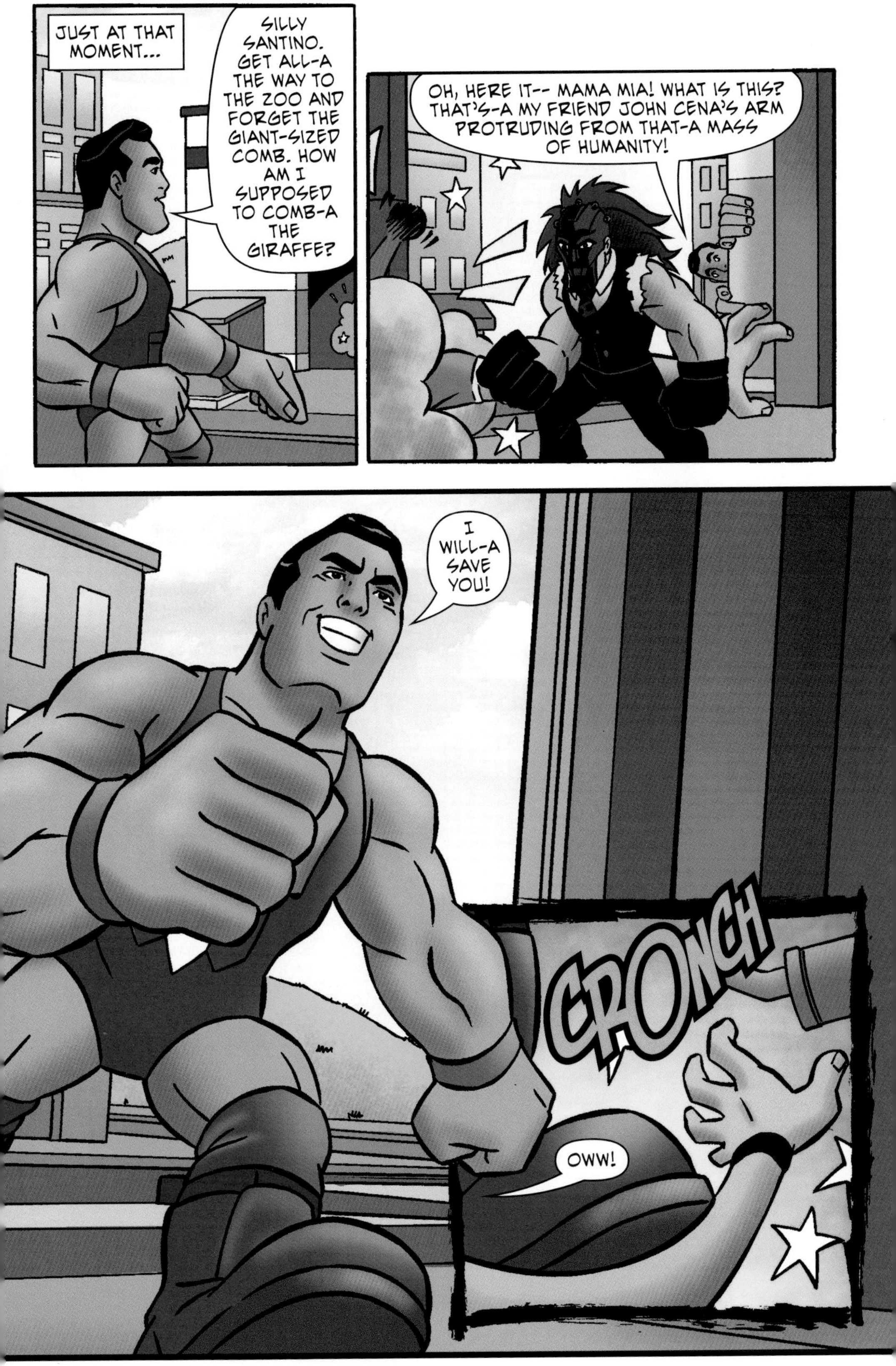
JUST AT THAT MOMENT...
SILLY SANTINO. GET ALL-A THE WAY TO THE ZOO AND FORGET THE GIANT-SIZED COMB. HOW AM I SUPPOSED TO COMB-A THE GIRAFFE?
OH, HERE IT-- MAMA MIA! WHAT IS THIS? THAT'S-A MY FRIEND JOHN CENA'S ARM PROTRUDING FROM THAT-A MASS OF HUMANITY!
I WILL-A SAVE YOU!
CRONCH
OWW!

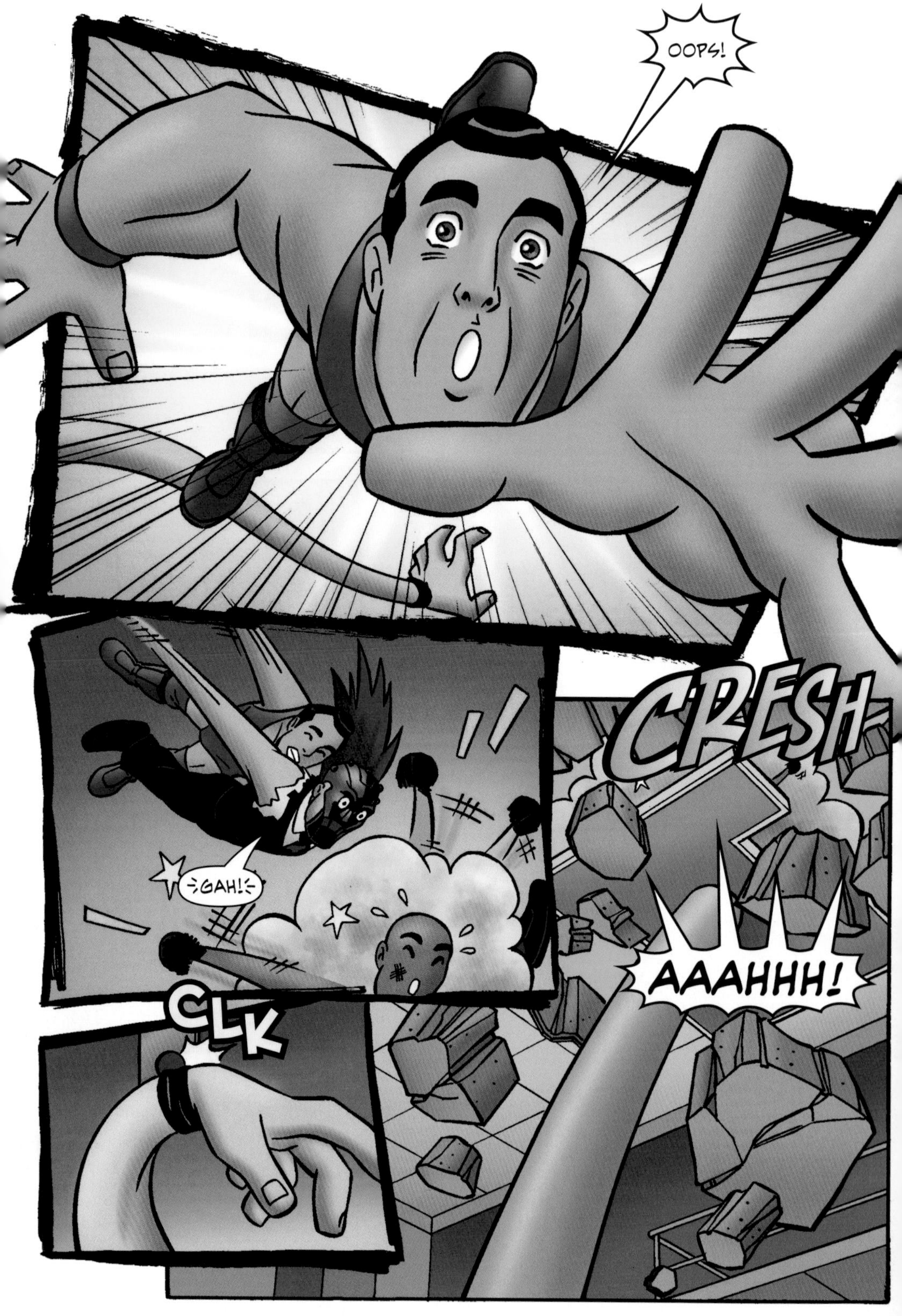
OOPS!
GAH!
CRESH
AAAHHH!
CLK

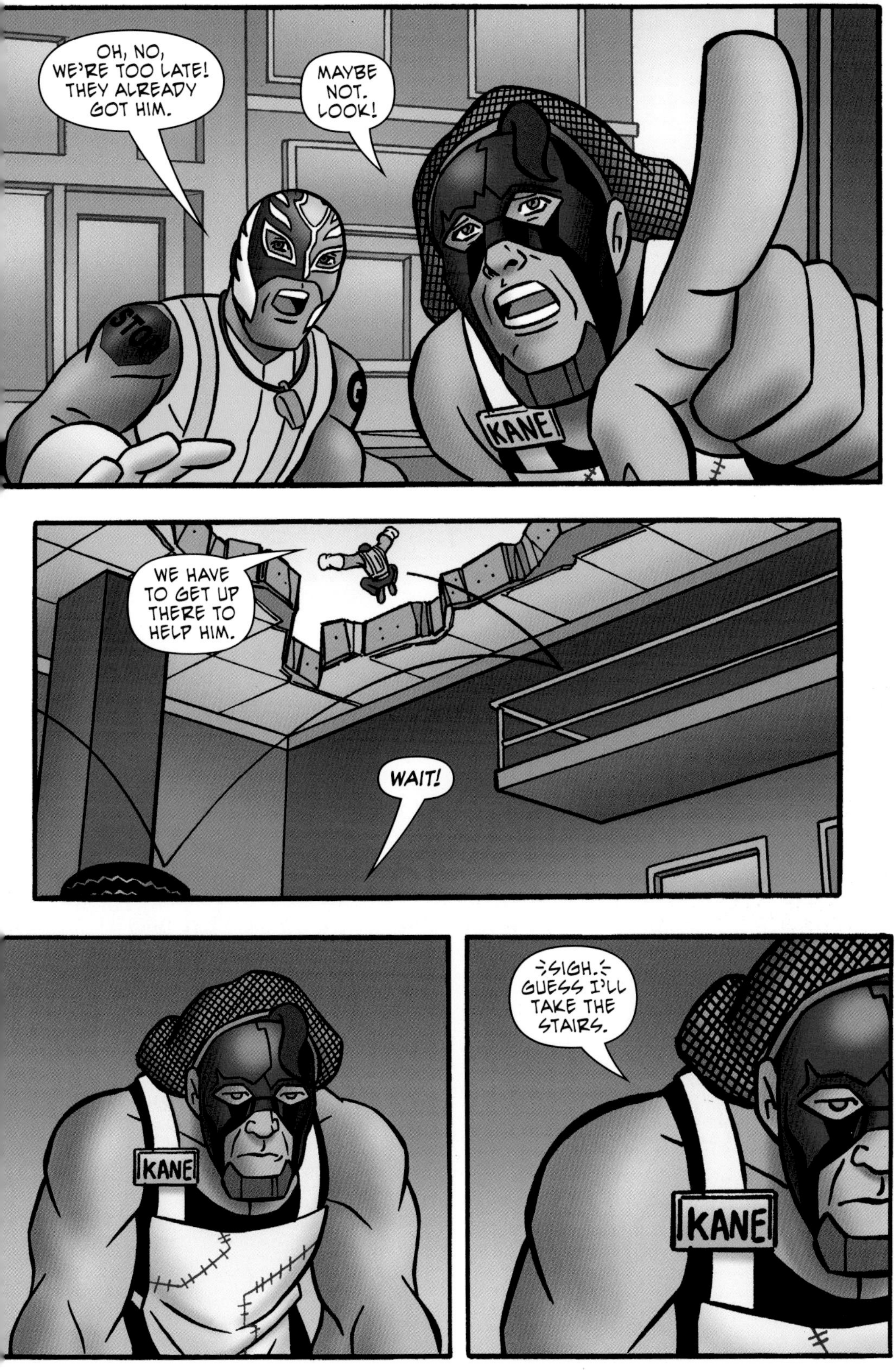
OH, NO, WE'RE TOO LATE! THEY ALREADY GOT HIM.
MAYBE NOT. LOOK!
STOP
G
KANE
WE HAVE TO GET UP THERE TO HELP HIM.
WAIT!
KANE
-SIGH.- GUESS I'LL TAKE THE STAIRS.
KANE

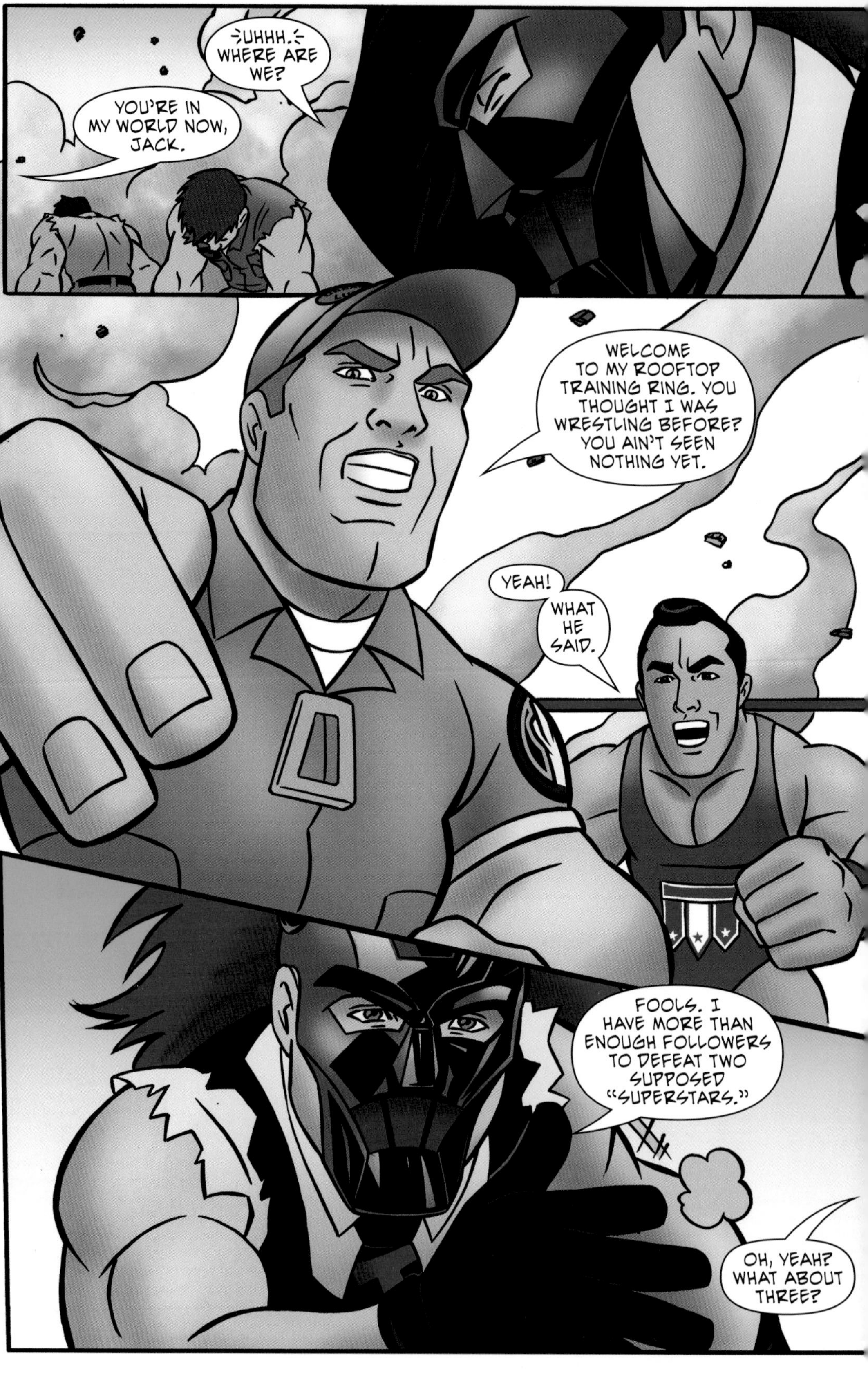
UHHH. WHERE ARE WE?
YOU'RE IN MY WORLD NOW, JACK.
WELCOME TO MY ROOFTOP TRAINING RING. YOU THOUGHT I WAS WRESTLING BEFORE? YOU AIN'T SEEN NOTHING YET.
YEAH!
WHAT HE SAID.
FOOLS. I HAVE MORE THAN ENOUGH FOLLOWERS TO DEFEAT TWO SUPPOSED "SUPERSTARS."
OH, YEAH? WHAT ABOUT THREE?

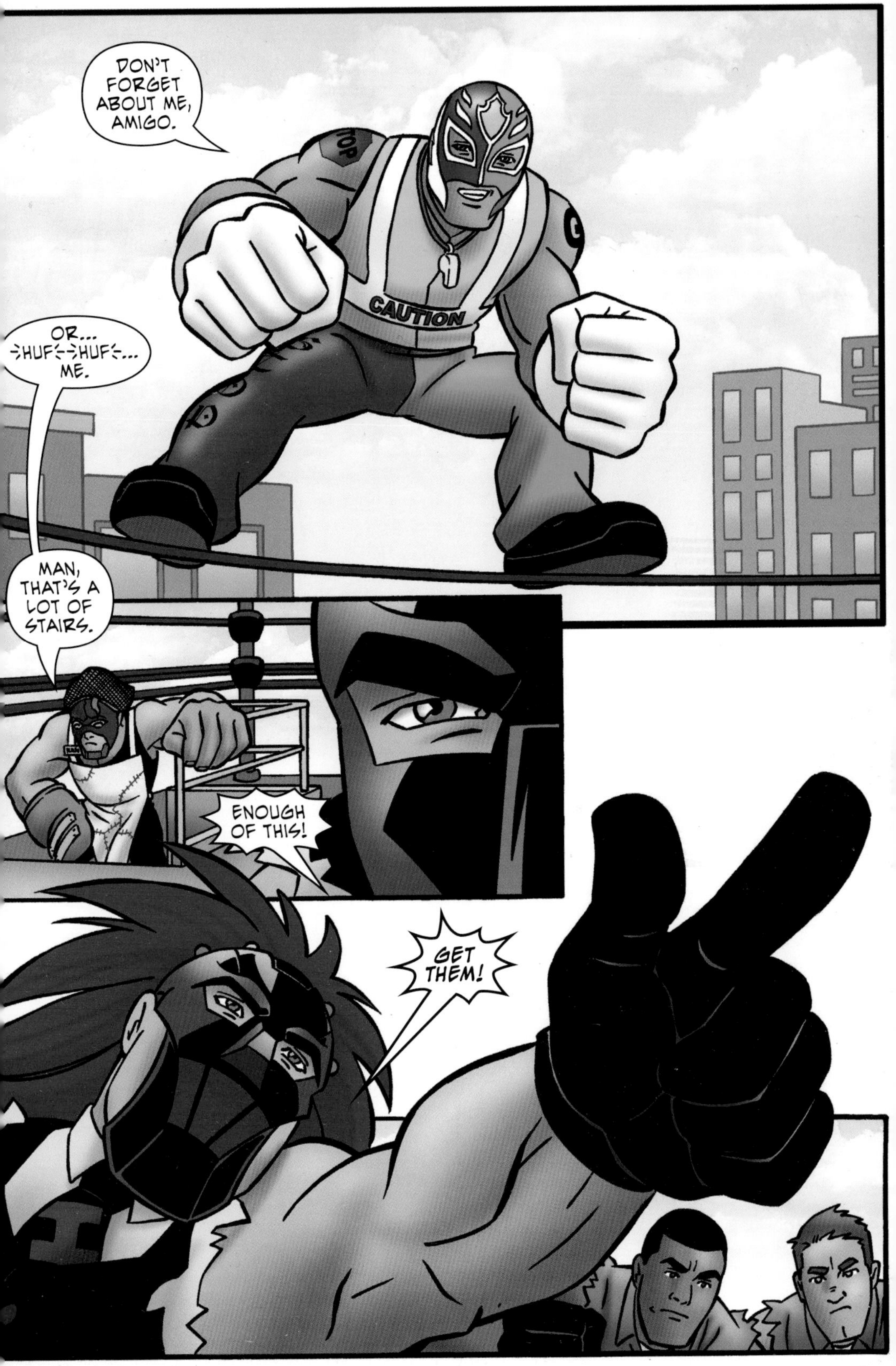
DON'T FORGET ABOUT ME, AMIGO.
CAUTION
OR... ~HUF~ ~HUF~... ME.
MAN, THAT'S A LOT OF STAIRS.
ENOUGH OF THIS!
GET THEM!

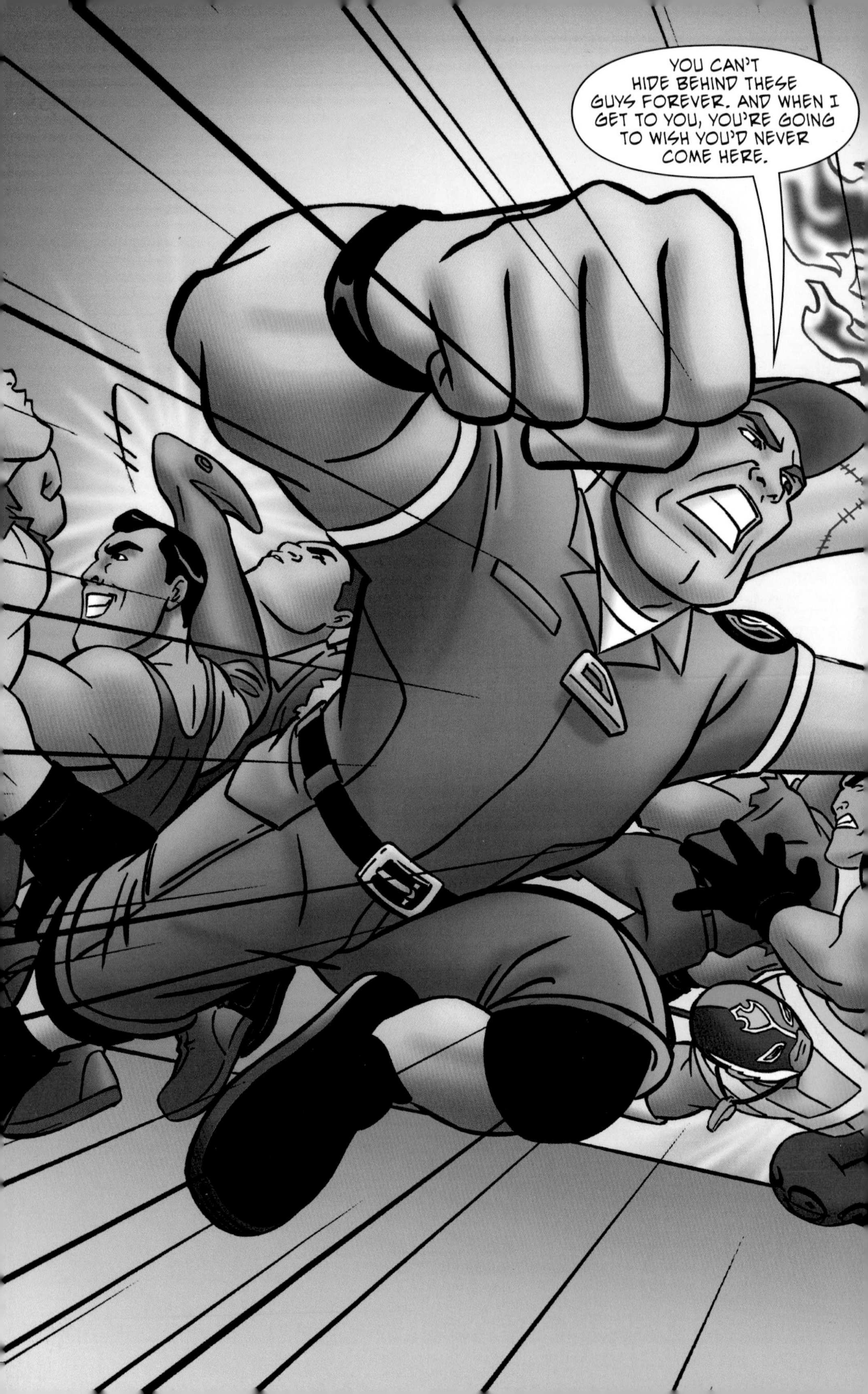
YOU CAN'T HIDE BEHIND THESE GUYS FOREVER. AND WHEN I GET TO YOU, YOU'RE GOING TO WISH YOU'D NEVER COME HERE.

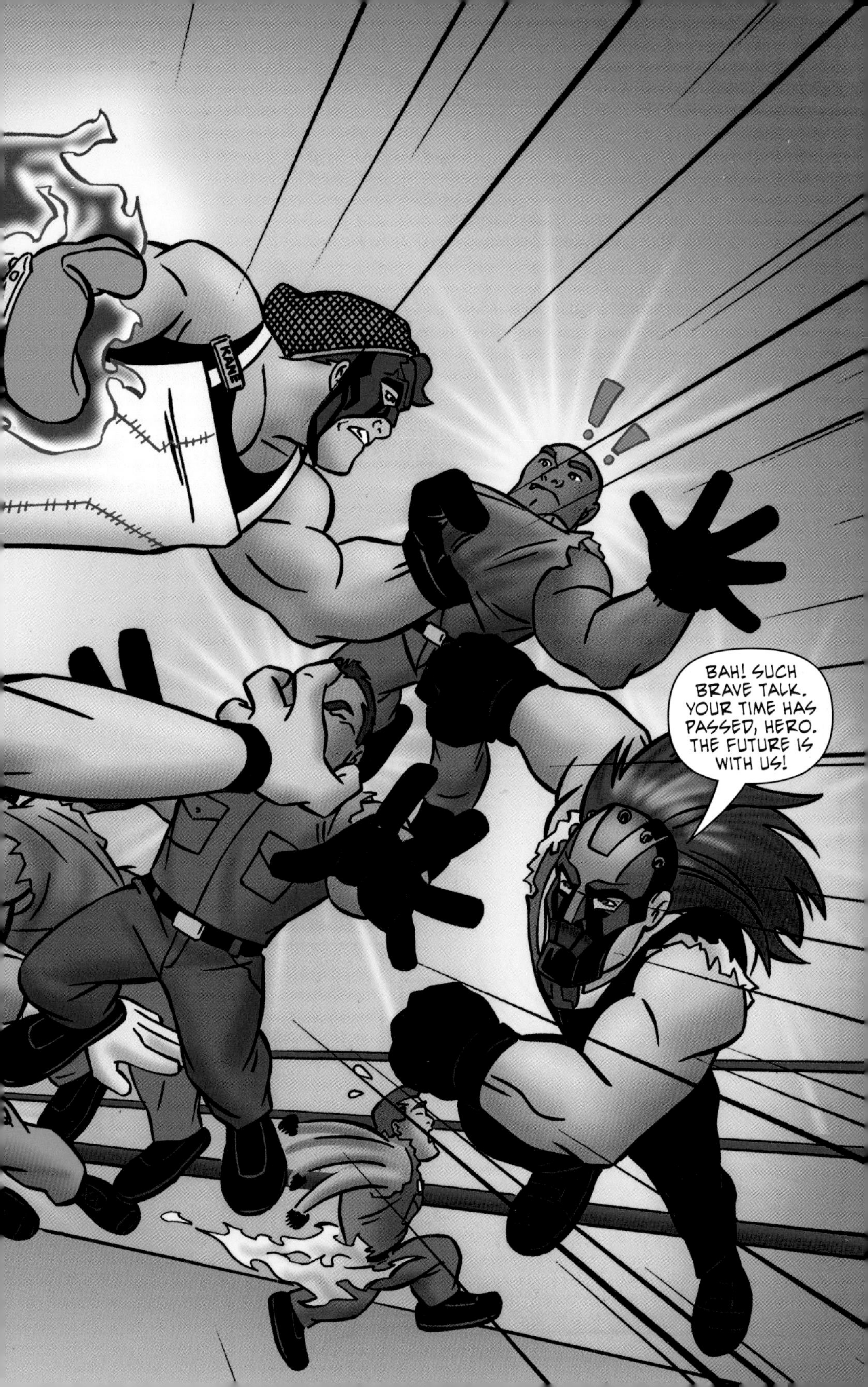
BAH! SUCH BRAVE TALK. YOUR TIME HAS PASSED, HERO. THE FUTURE IS WITH US!
KANE

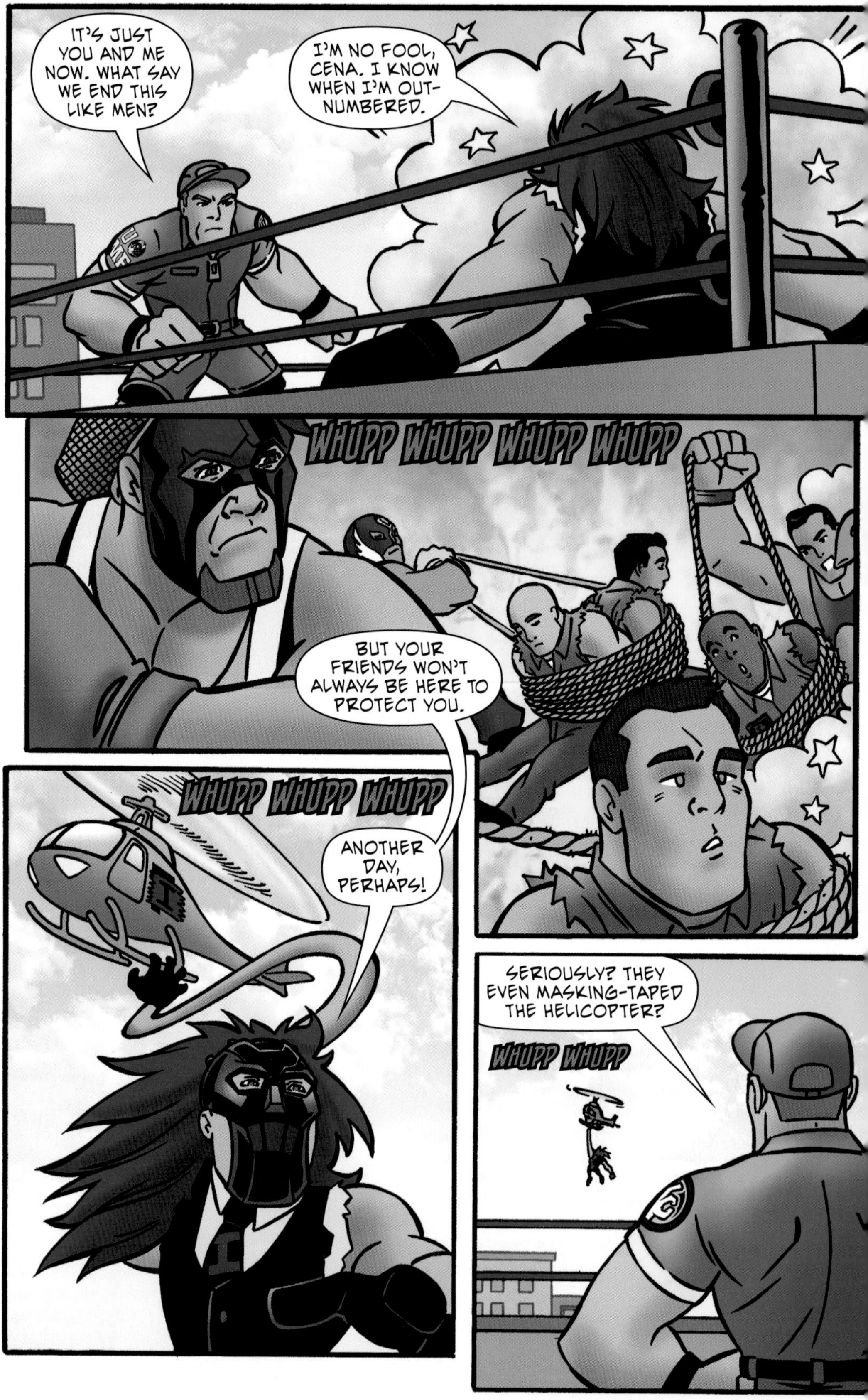
IT'S JUST YOU AND ME NOW. WHAT SAY WE END THIS LIKE MEN?
I'M NO FOOL, CENA. I KNOW WHEN I'M OUT-NUMBERED.
WHUPP WHUPP WHUPP WHUPP
BUT YOUR FRIENDS WON'T ALWAYS BE HERE TO PROTECT YOU.
WHUPP WHUPP WHUPP
ANOTHER DAY, PERHAPS!
SERIOUSLY? THEY EVEN MASKING-TAPED THE HELICOPTER?
WHUPP WHUPP

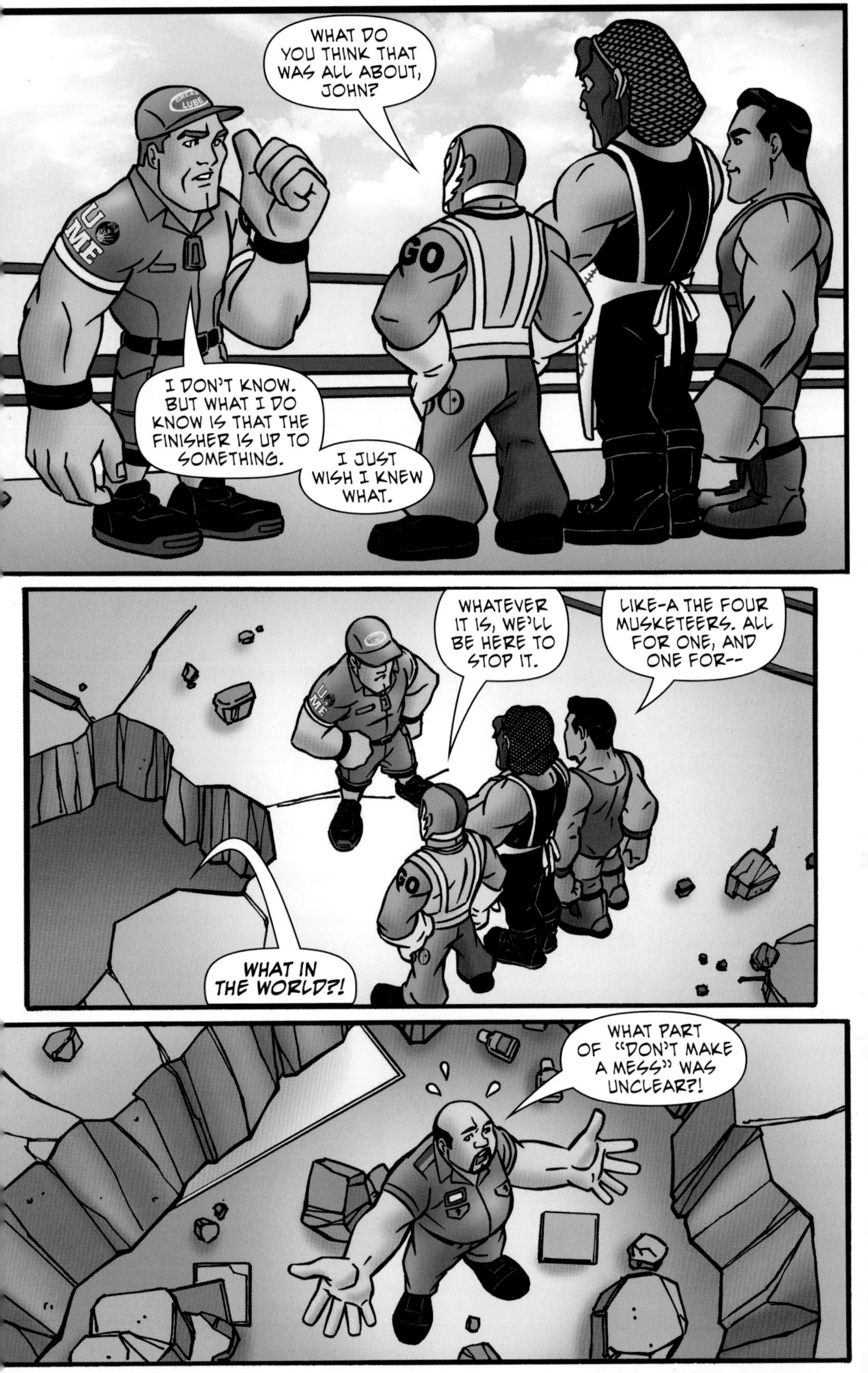
WHAT DO YOU THINK THAT WAS ALL ABOUT, JOHN?
I DON'T KNOW. BUT WHAT I DO KNOW IS THAT THE FINISHER IS UP TO SOMETHING.
I JUST WISH I KNEW WHAT.
WHATEVER IT IS, WE'LL BE HERE TO STOP IT.
LIKE-A THE FOUR MUSKETEERS. ALL FOR ONE, AND ONE FOR--
WHAT IN THE WORLD?!
WHAT PART OF "DON'T MAKE A MESS" WAS UNCLEAR?!

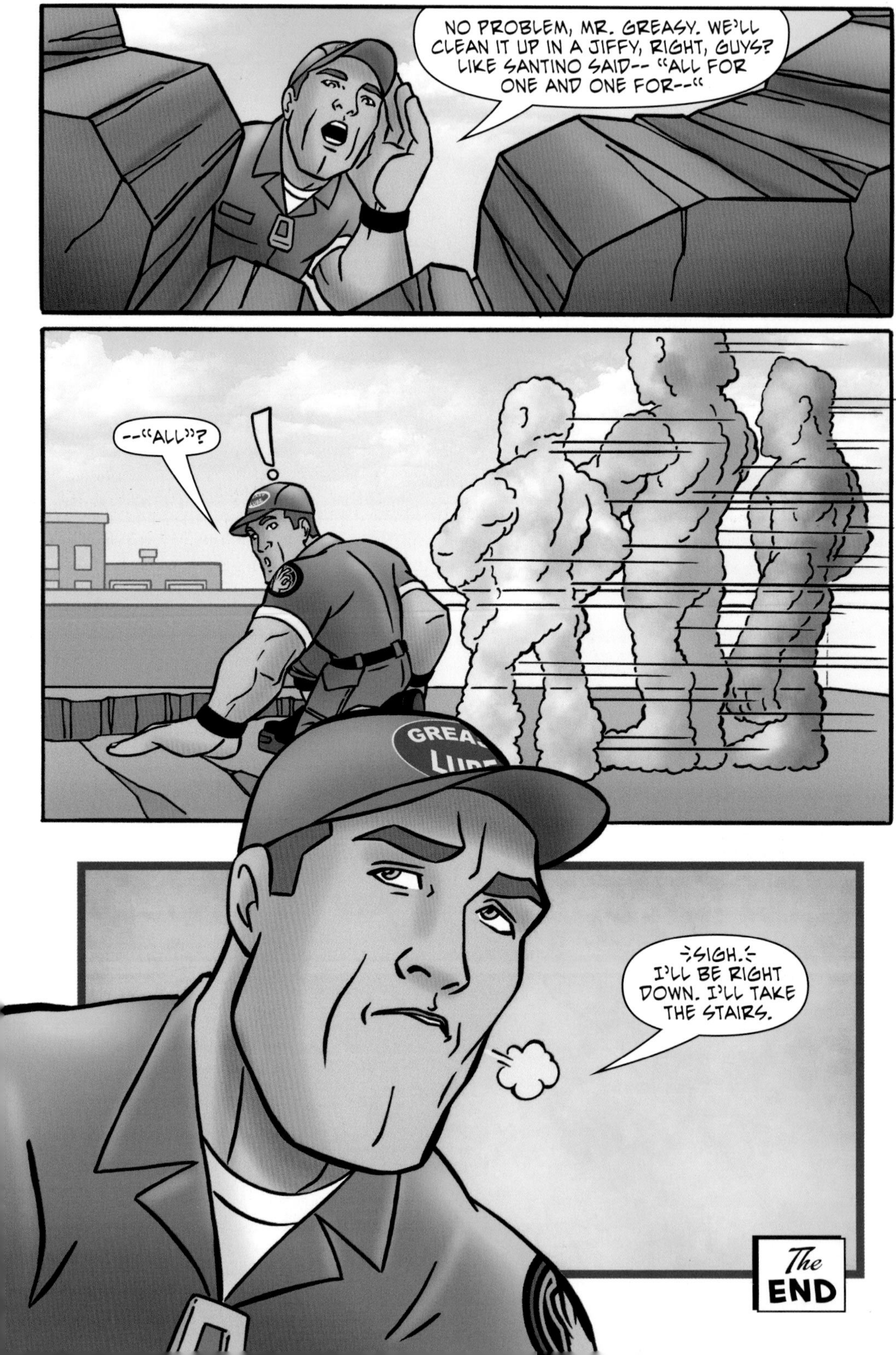
NO PROBLEM, MR. GREASY. WE'LL CLEAN IT UP IN A JIFFY, RIGHT, GUYS? LIKE SANTINO SAID-- "ALL FOR ONE AND ONE FOR--"
--"ALL"?
!
GREASY LUBE
SIGH. I'LL BE RIGHT DOWN. I'LL TAKE THE STAIRS.
The END

WATCH OUT FOR PAPERCUTZ

Welcome to power-packed, premiere WWE SLAM CITY graphic novel from Papercutz, those pencil-neck geeks who are dedicated to publishing great graphic novels for all ages! I'm Jim Salicrup, the Editor-in-Chief and retired SLAM CITY referee.

It's been a real thrill putting this all-new graphic novel together, based on the WWE SLAM CITY animated short films that have been playing all over the world-wide web! The WWE SLAM CITY creative crew has been a real pleasure to work with, but there was one odd aspect to that I'd like to share with you. You see, our writer is something of an enigma. In fact, I haven't actually met him in-person, and he tends to be rather secretive. Anxious to learn more about him, we asked him to send us a short bio that we could post here to share with the WWE Universe. Here it is…

"Who is Mathias Triton? Hero or villain? Champ or chump? No one knows for sure. This man of mystery claims to be a New York Times best-selling author, an accomplished graphic novel writer, and the only man ever to beat Andre the Giant in a fair fight. But which of these facts are true? Perhaps all. Perhaps none. The only thing we know for sure is that he has his checks sent directly to a one-man bank in Gammesfeld, Germany."

That bio actually raises more questions than it answers. I mean, I have enough problems trying to figure out who the Instigator is. Fortunately, I do know who Alitha E. Martinez is! She's the artist who did such an awesome job illustrating the first four issues of the WWE SUPERSTARS comicbook from Super Genius, a Papercutz imprint. All four issues have been collected into a trade paperback called WWE SUPERSTARS #1 "Money in the Bank!" and is available now at booksellers everywhere for just $9.99! It features all your favorite WWE Superstars in a story that shows them in a way you've never seen them before—as characters in a noir thriller. Alitha did such an amazing job drawing so many WWE superstars, and their signature moves, that we couldn't think of anyone better qualified to draw WWE SLAM CITY! (Somehow, Alitha managed to find enough time in her busy schedule to do a very special sequence, as well as the cover to issue #7 of WWE SUPERSTARS. It's in yet another style than we've already seen from this talented artist!)

We're also lucky to know who JayJay Jackson and Tom Orzechowski are—they also worked away on WWE SUPERSTARS, handling the coloring and lettering respectively. When you have such top talents available, why look for anyone else? So, we're thrilled to have them work on WWE SLAM CITY as well!

We're all having such fun on this graphic novel, we're going to do it all over again! That's right, this is not just a one-shot, but an on-going series of WWE SLAM CITY graphic novels! Up next is "WWE SLAM CITY #2 "Rise of El Diablo"! Just to whet your appetite, we're featuring a special preview on the following pages—so check it out! In the meantime, let us know what you thought WWE SLAM CITY #1! You can reach us via the contacts listed in the box below!

So until we meet again, as one of my favorite sports entertainers often says…

Have a nice day! Jim

STAY IN TOUCH!

EMAIL:	salicrup@papercutz.com
WEB:	papercutz.com
TWITTER:	@papercutzgn
FACEBOOK:	PAPERCUTZGRAPHICNOVELS
FAN MAIL:	Papercutz, 160 Broadway, Suite 700, East Wing, New York, NY 10038

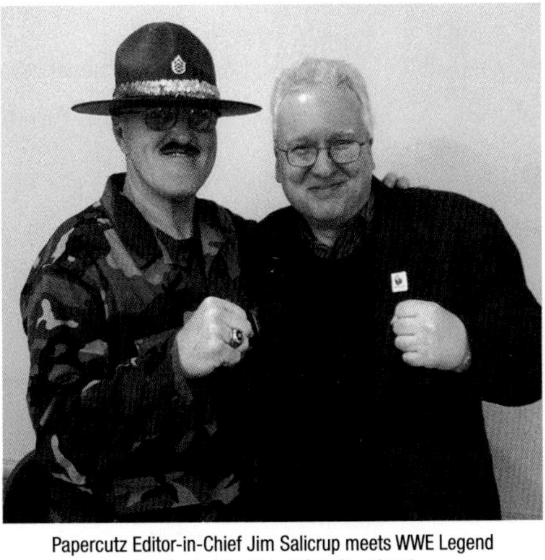

Papercutz Editor-in-Chief Jim Salicrup meets WWE Legend (and erstwhile GI Joe) Sgt. Slaughter!

IT'S PASS GO TIME!

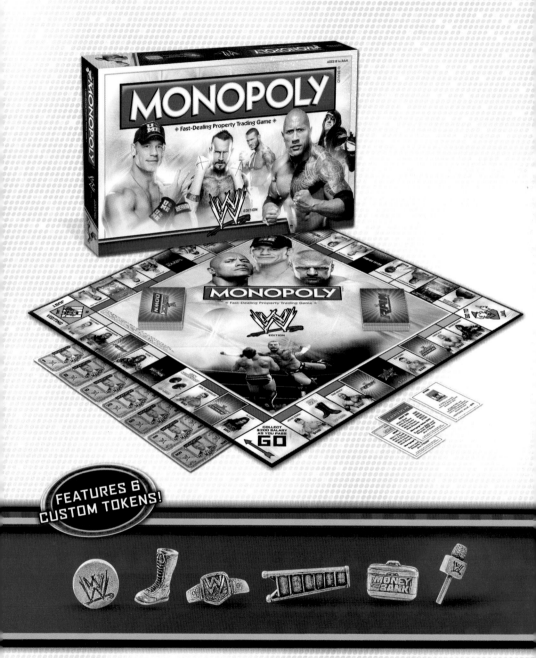

FEATURES 6 CUSTOM TOKENS!

AVAILABLE NOW AT WWE.COM AND AMAZON.COM

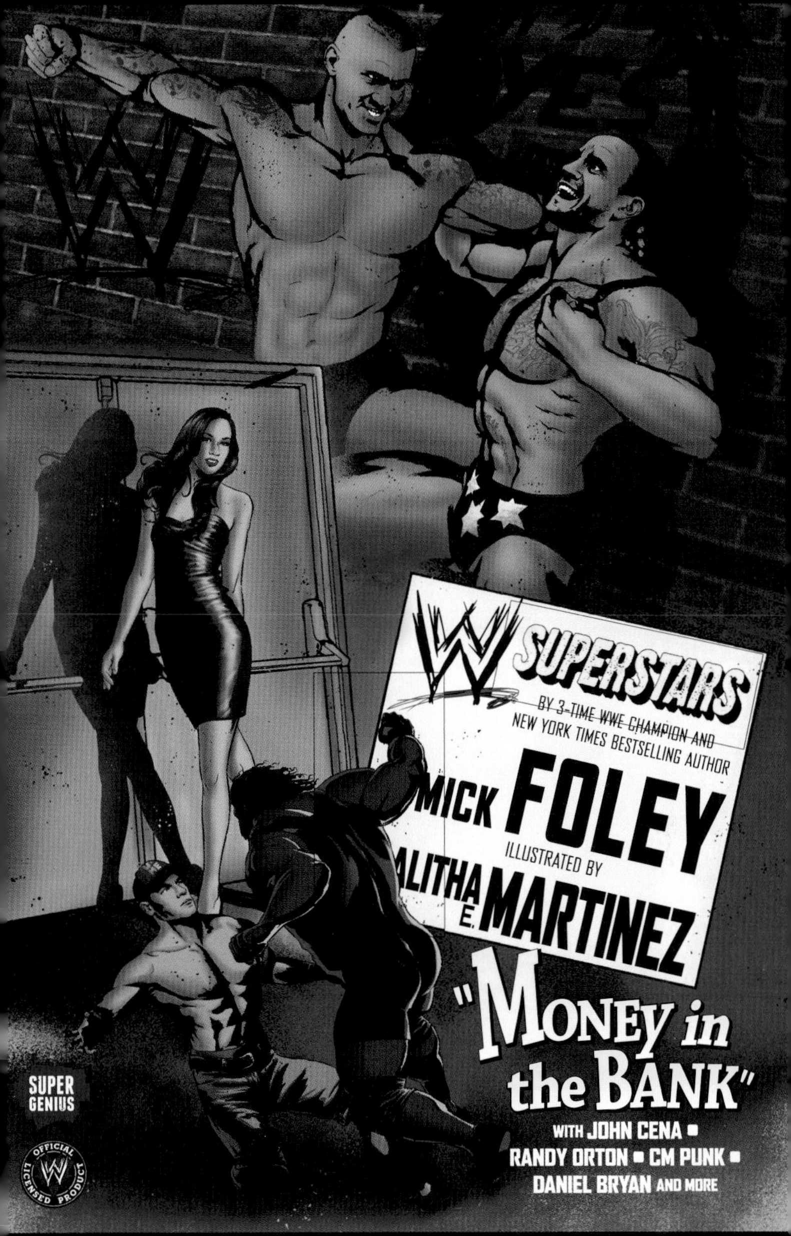
SUPERSTARS
BY 3-TIME WWE CHAMPION AND
NEW YORK TIMES BESTSELLING AUTHOR
MICK FOLEY
ILLUSTRATED BY
ALITHA E. MARTINEZ
"MONEY in the BANK"
WITH JOHN CENA • RANDY ORTON • CM PUNK • DANIEL BRYAN AND MORE
SUPER GENIUS
OFFICIAL LICENSED PRODUCT

PROMOTION

SUBSCRIBE NOW! SAVE 65% OFF THE NEWSSTAND SALE PRICE

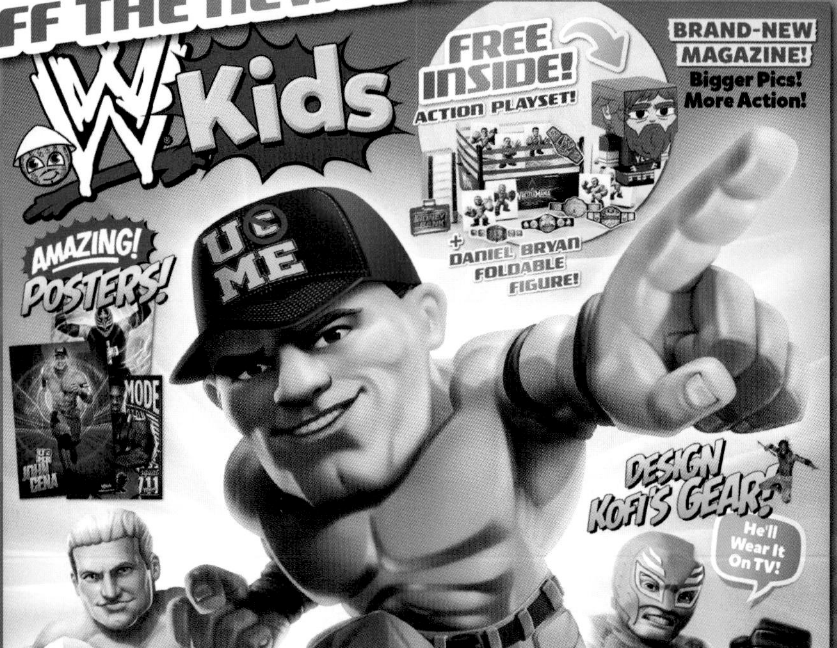
WWE Kids
FREE INSIDE!
ACTION PLAYSET!
+ DANIEL BRYAN FOLDABLE FIGURE!
BRAND-NEW MAGAZINE!
Bigger Pics! More Action!
AMAZING! POSTERS!
U C ME
DESIGN KOFI'S GEAR!
He'll Wear It On TV!
DZ
DOLPH ZIGGLER
JOHN CENA
BUILD A MEGA POSTER! START NOW!
IMPRESS MOM! Three Brain Blowing Tricks! Page 3
EAT STRONG! Scarf Like A Superstar! Page 29
1 YEAR (10 ISSUES) FOR ONLY $19.95

AWESOME POSTERS! FANTASTIC PRIZES! SUPERSTAR INTERVIEWS! FOLDABLE FIGURES!

GO TO: MAG.WWEKIDS.COM

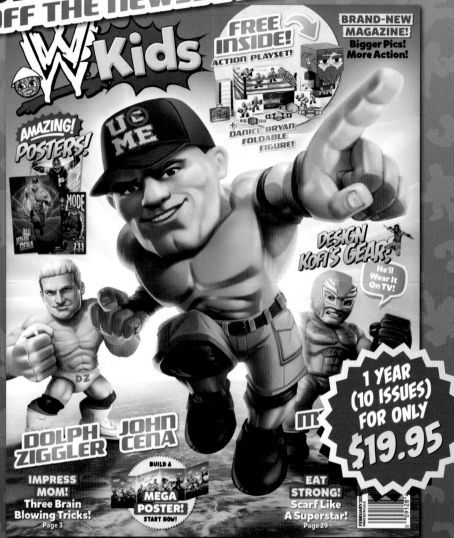

Special Preview of WWE SLAM CITY #2 "Rise of El Diablo"

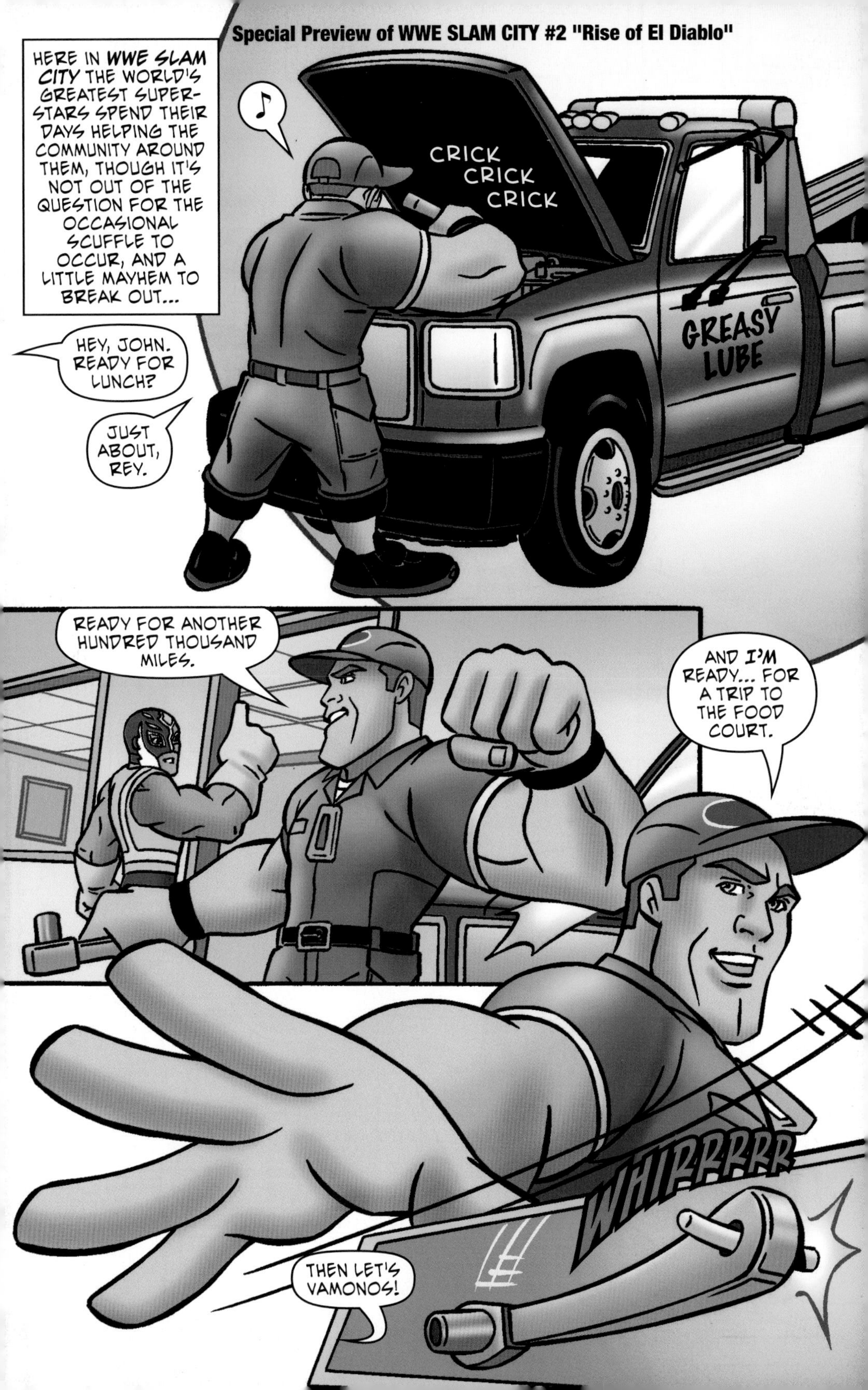
HERE IN *WWE SLAM CITY* THE WORLD'S GREATEST SUPER-STARS SPEND THEIR DAYS HELPING THE COMMUNITY AROUND THEM, THOUGH IT'S NOT OUT OF THE QUESTION FOR THE OCCASIONAL SCUFFLE TO OCCUR, AND A LITTLE MAYHEM TO BREAK OUT...
♪
CRICK CRICK CRICK
GREASY LUBE
HEY, JOHN. READY FOR LUNCH?
JUST ABOUT, REY.
READY FOR ANOTHER HUNDRED THOUSAND MILES.
AND I'M READY... FOR A TRIP TO THE FOOD COURT.
THEN LET'S VAMONOS!
WHIRRRRR

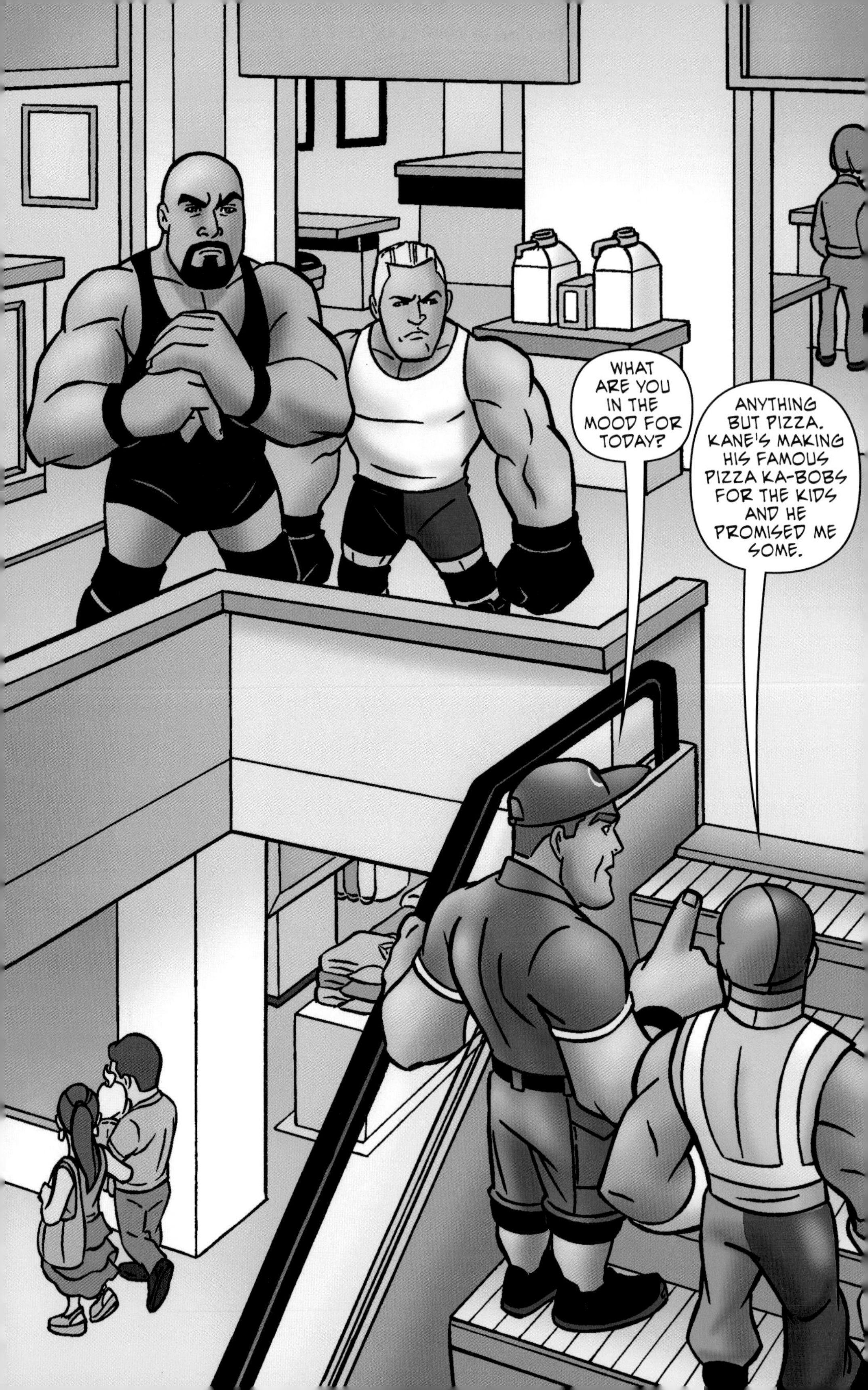
WHAT ARE YOU IN THE MOOD FOR TODAY?
ANYTHING BUT PIZZA. KANE'S MAKING HIS FAMOUS PIZZA KA-BOBS FOR THE KIDS AND HE PROMISED ME SOME.

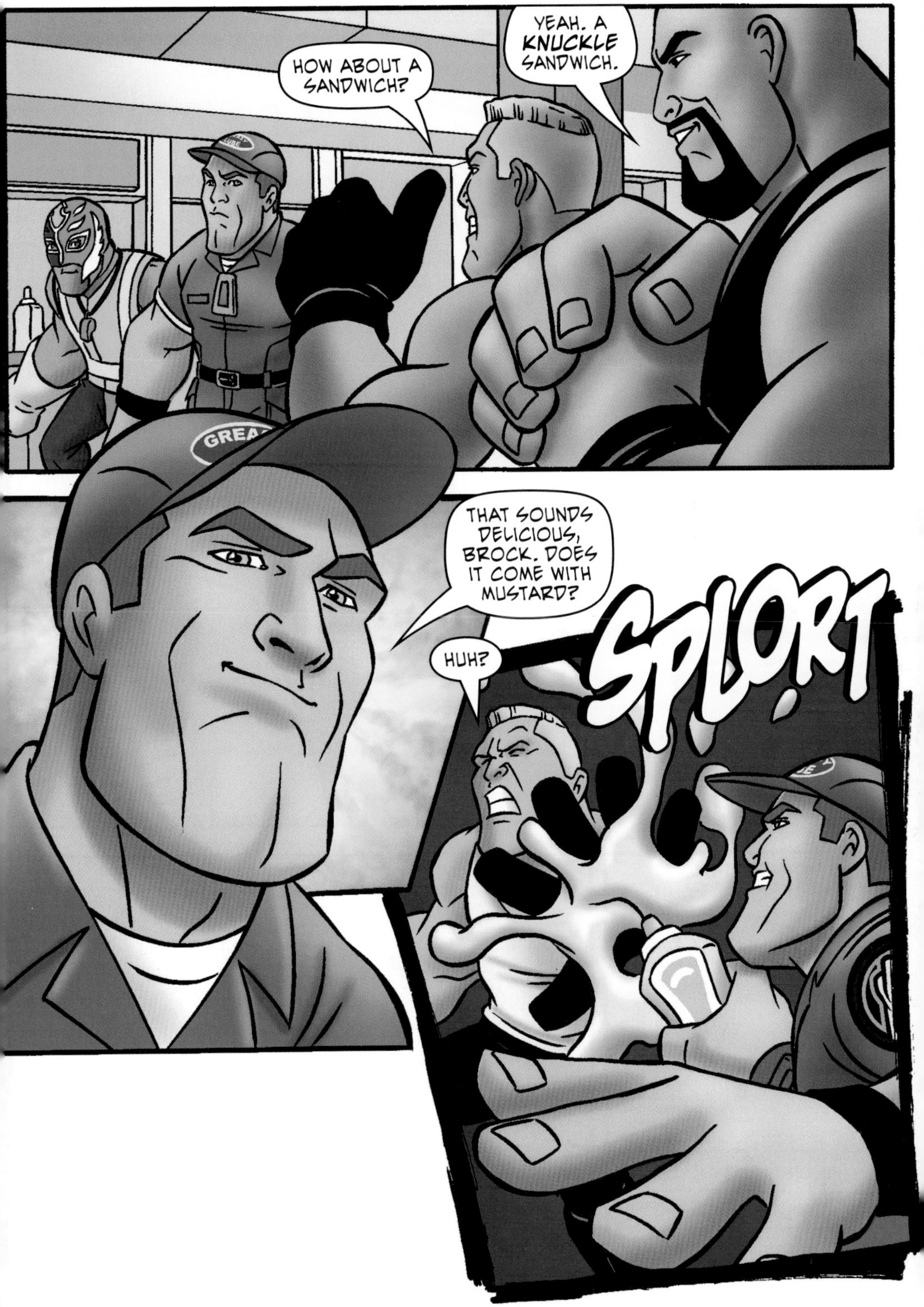
HOW ABOUT A SANDWICH?
YEAH. A KNUCKLE SANDWICH.
THAT SOUNDS DELICIOUS, BROCK. DOES IT COME WITH MUSTARD?
HUH?
SPLORT

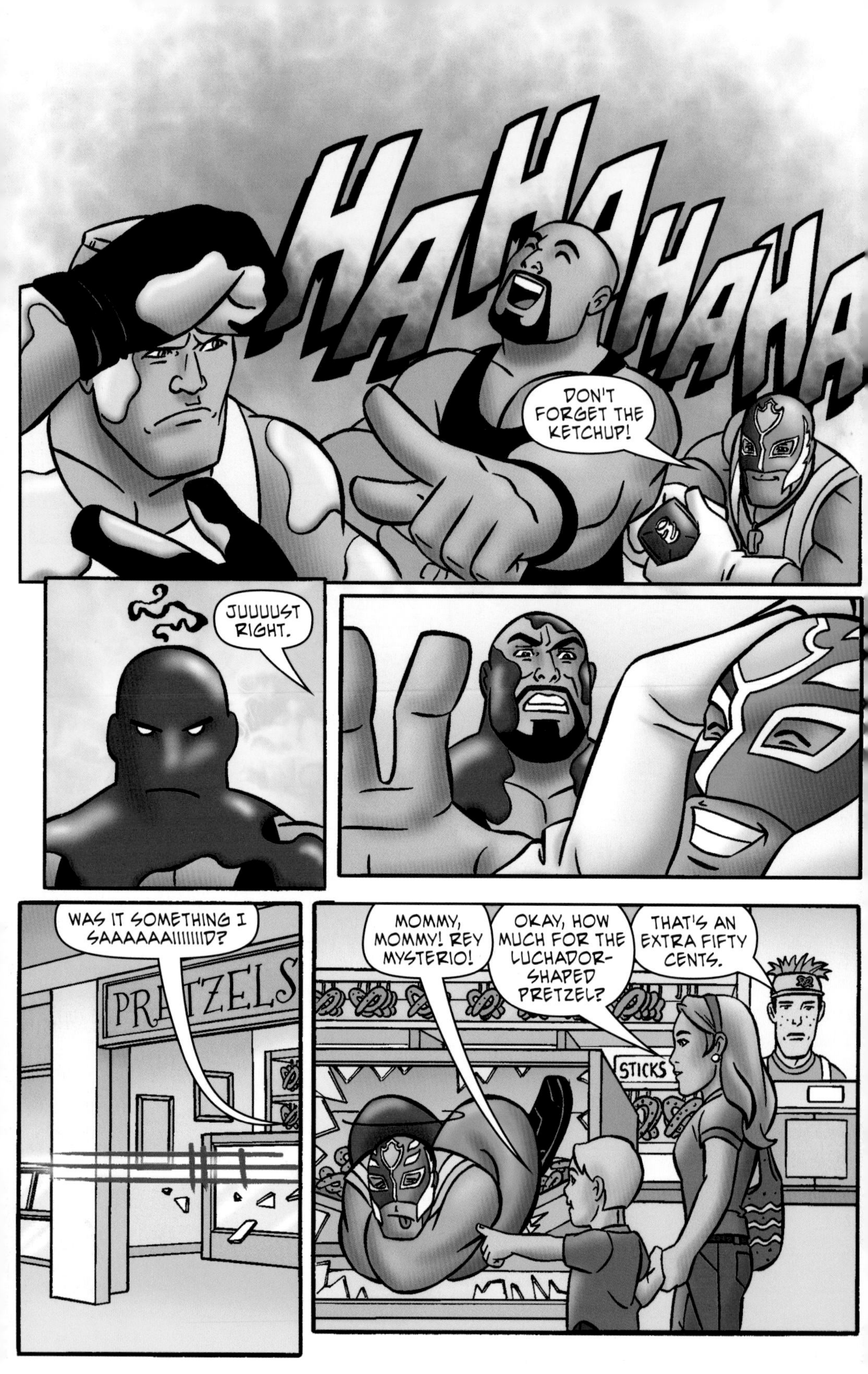

HAHAHAHA
DON'T FORGET THE KETCHUP!
JUUUUST RIGHT.
WAS IT SOMETHING I SAAAAAAIIIIIIID?
PRETZELS
MOMMY, MOMMY! REY MYSTERIO!
OKAY, HOW MUCH FOR THE LUCHADOR-SHAPED PRETZEL?
THAT'S AN EXTRA FIFTY CENTS.
STICKS

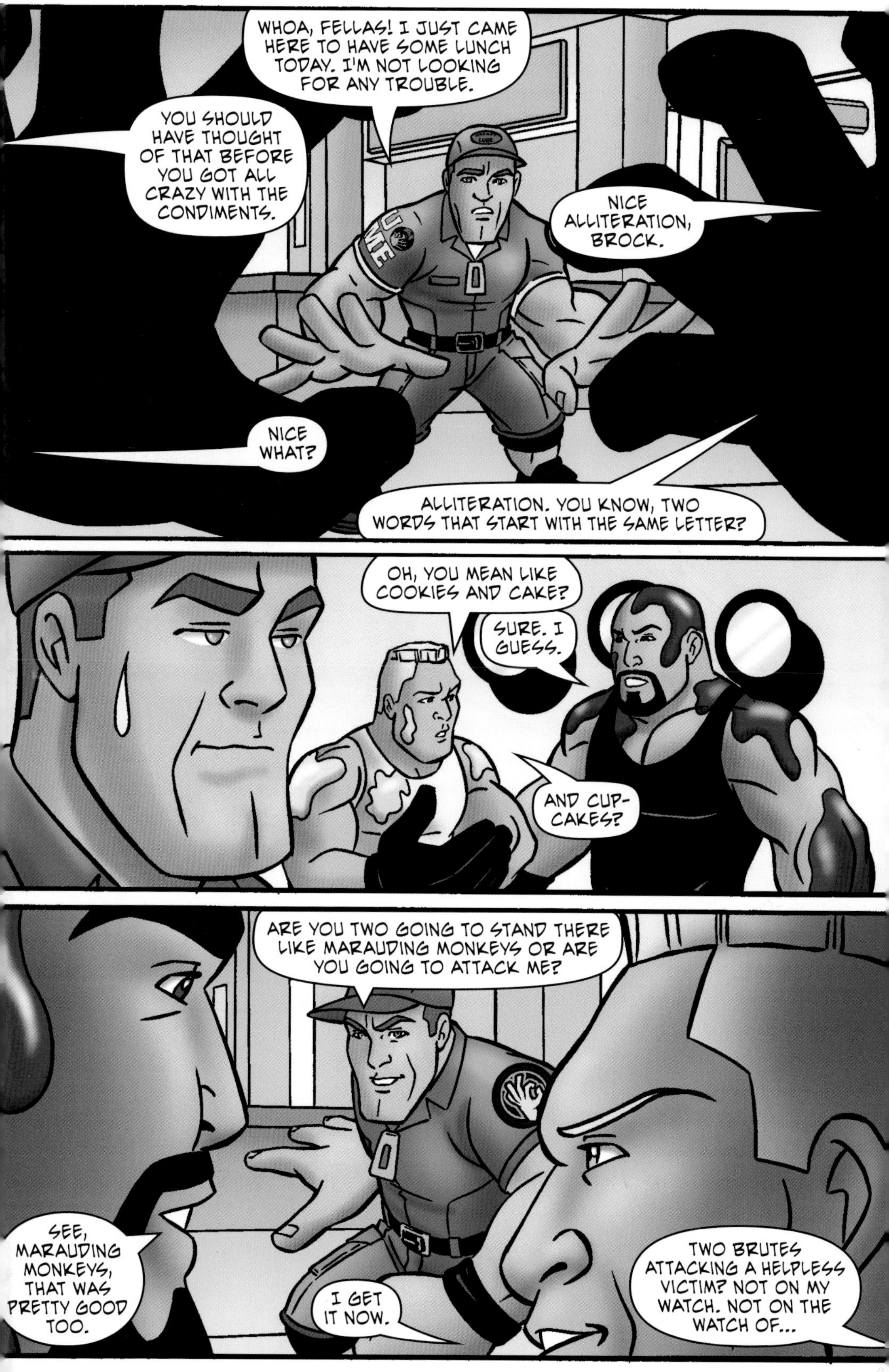
WHOA, FELLAS! I JUST CAME HERE TO HAVE SOME LUNCH TODAY. I'M NOT LOOKING FOR ANY TROUBLE.
YOU SHOULD HAVE THOUGHT OF THAT BEFORE YOU GOT ALL CRAZY WITH THE CONDIMENTS.
NICE ALLITERATION, BROCK.
NICE WHAT?
ALLITERATION. YOU KNOW, TWO WORDS THAT START WITH THE SAME LETTER?
OH, YOU MEAN LIKE COOKIES AND CAKE?
SURE. I GUESS.
AND CUP-CAKES?
ARE YOU TWO GOING TO STAND THERE LIKE MARAUDING MONKEYS OR ARE YOU GOING TO ATTACK ME?
SEE, MARAUDING MONKEYS, THAT WAS PRETTY GOOD TOO.
I GET IT NOW.
TWO BRUTES ATTACKING A HELPLESS VICTIM? NOT ON MY WATCH. NOT ON THE WATCH OF...

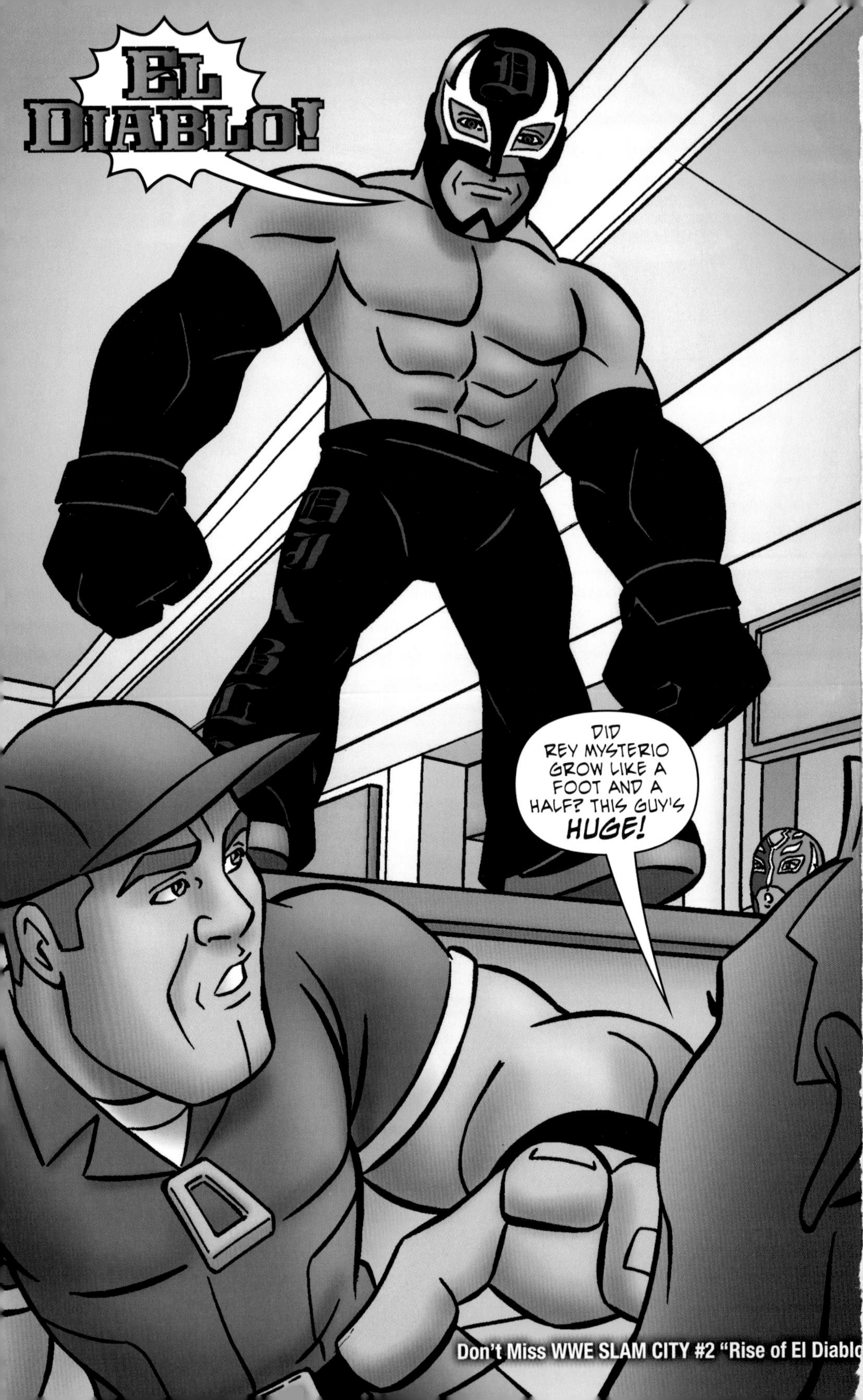
EL DIABLO!
DID REY MYSTERIO GROW LIKE A FOOT AND A HALF? THIS GUY'S HUGE!
Don't Miss WWE SLAM CITY #2 "Rise of El Diablo